ANTIGEN:

Love and War, Book 2

R. A. STEFFAN

INTRODUCTION

This book contains graphic violence and explicit sexual content. It is intended for a mature audience. While it is part of a series with an overarching plot, it can be read as a standalone with a happy ending for the two main characters, and a satisfying resolution of the storyline.

TABLE OF CONTENTS

ONE

"Put down the protoplaser and raise your hands where we can see them, Frey Erisuel," said the armed guard standing in the doorway of the prison infirmary.

The woman leaning over Temple's naked torso tensed, and Temple hissed out a breath as the medical instrument she was running over the sluggishly bleeding gash in his chest slipped, stinging the ragged edges of the wound. Very carefully, the Vithii doctor shut the device off and set it aside, straightening but not turning around.

One of the prison sub-intendants had ordered Temple to be taken to the infirmary after he'd been beaten and shivved in the exercise yard. It wasn't the worst injury he'd gotten since being captured, and it also wasn't the first time they'd sent him here to be patched up. It was, however, the first time he'd been seen by this particular doctor. She'd gruffly informed him that it was her fourth day on the job, and that she was replacing one of the older doctors who had just retired.

Now, she was apparently about to be arrested.

Any deviation from the norm inside the prison was generally a cause for worry if you happened to be an inmate, so Temple held his breath as he waited to see what would happen next. Because the woman was Vithii, they *probably* wouldn't shoot her down in cold blood—but in this place, assumptions like that could be dangerous.

"My name is Dr. Radathian," she said in a level voice, though Temple could see the tendons in her jaw standing out as she held herself completely still. "I don't know anyone named Erisuel. What is this about? I have a patient here who needs treatment."

The guard stepped further inside the room, allowing space for three other uniformed Vithii to enter and flank him. They stood with their hands on their sidearms, but did not draw them. Temple wondered what the hell was going on, and how likely he was to end up getting dragged into it. He'd been stuck in this stinking hole for almost a month now. At least, he thought it was almost a month. He'd been sick for several days shortly after he was captured, and time in this place tended to run together into a continuous blur if you didn't pay attention carefully.

The guard gestured with his sidearm, even though the red-haired Vithii woman still hadn't turned around. "Your name is Aryderlyn Erisuel, and you are under arrest for several charges, including child endangerment, illegal use of nanotech, obtaining government employment using a false identity, and practicing medicine without a license. At least one of those is a capital crime. You're coming with us."

For a moment, Temple wondered if the doctor would try to make a fight of things. It would be hopeless, he was sure, but the tension in her body spoke of someone hovering on the knife-edge of the fight-or-flight response. A brief flash of desperation or insanity made Temple wonder if the two of them together could somehow overpower four armed guards and get away. Fortunately, good sense kicked in before he could make a mistake that would probably be fatal for both of them.

An instant later, some of the tension left the woman's rigid posture, and he knew she'd given up on the idea as well. "You've made a mistake," she said, "but I'll come with you so I can get it sorted out with your superior."

"There's no mistake, Frey Erisuel," the guard insisted. "Now turn around slowly, and keep your hands in plain view."

Temple saw the doctor's jaw clench, but he noticed she didn't protest being addressed as *Frey*—the Vithii equivalent of *Ms.* or *ma'am*—rather than *Doctor*. Having been on her exam table for some time before the guards had barged in, he was pretty confident she did, in fact, have extensive medical training. He thought all his curiosity should have been pretty much beaten out of him by this point, but he still couldn't help wondering what the story was here.

Just worry about whether or not you'll get sucked into this mess, he tried to tell himself. *What do you care about some Regime lackey anyway?*

The answer was that he didn't—even if she *had* been professional and competent in her dealings with him as she treated the fallout from his latest round of 'accidental' injuries.

She turned around slowly, as instructed, her lips pressed into a thin line. She was striking, as far as Vithii women went, with her spiky hair dyed a vibrant shade of red and her large brown eyes full of fire.

"This inmate needs further treatment," she said through gritted teeth. "Let me finish what I was doing, or at least call someone else to take over my shift in the infirmary. I'm the only doctor on duty."

The guard snorted. "Then there's *no* doctor on duty, is there?" he jerked his chin toward the guards standing on his left. "Take the human prisoner back to his cell. He looks fine."

"Yes, sir," the larger one barked.

Temple rolled slowly into a sitting position, careful not to make any movements that could conceivably be interpreted as threatening. The guards in the capital city prison had a unique definition of what constituted *fine*, at least when it came to the human inmates. He was painfully aware of the way his half-healed wound gaped at the bottom edge, another little trickle of blood oozing out to drip down his chest as he rose.

The woman's eyes cut to his briefly. "Try to keep it clean," she said. "The shiv didn't penetrate deeply enough to hit anything vital, and the broad-spectrum antibiotic injection should hold infection at bay. I'll try to arrange for you to come back in as soon as this is sorted out."

"That's enough talking," the guard said, sounding bored.

He and one of his colleagues came forward and took the woman by the arms, marching her out of the room. The shorter of the remaining two guards grabbed Temple by the bicep, and shoved him hard toward the door. Temple staggered, his chest flaring in pain as the abrupt movement pulled against the wound, but he managed to right himself and follow the guards' prodding, heading back toward the empty box they called a cell.

Behind him, one of the goons snickered. "Heard that bitch was bonded to one of the higher-ups in the Regime," he said to his companion. "He dropped her like a hot *faroa* root when he found out what she really was. She's gonna be *so* fucked now."

The other guard barked a laugh. "Fucked? Not likely, if she's *grei'kaapt*. Ugh. Even the thought makes my skin crawl. Wonder what possessed her to sneak into this place with a fake identity?"

"Who knows? Maybe she's suicidal."

"Pfft. That's a pretty fuckin' convoluted suicide plan. Nah. You mark my words. There's something else going on. The shit's gettin' sucked into the turbo intake as we speak. Just gotta make sure not to be standing behind the exhaust port when it sprays out, right?"

"Ain't that the truth."

Temple kept his head down and did what was expected of him as they trudged along the endless corridors in the belly of the prison complex. It was all well and good telling himself that he didn't give a rat's ass for the mysterious Vithii woman who'd upended the normal order of things in this strictly regimented little kingdom. But that didn't stop him from mulling over this new information with interest.

Maybe his brain was just desperate for some kind of intellectual stimulation. A puzzle to solve.

The guard was right, though. What in the name of sanity would possess a Vithii woman who was wanted on criminal charges to risk herself by entering a Regime prison using a fake identity? Especially a woman who used to be bonded to a Regime official? Most wives of government higher-ups were simpering things whose only function appeared to be looking pretty and vacuous while hanging on their husbands' arms.

It was a hard image to reconcile with a woman who'd stared down four armed guards like she was considering tearing them limb from limb. She'd been afraid, yes, but all she'd offered the guards was a stubborn jaw and a flat, challenging gaze.

Gods and prophets, was he already succumbing to that thing Skye had told him about back when she was attending university, stuck in a psychology class that she hadn't wanted to take? *Stockholm Syndrome*, or whatever it was called?

Because he was getting seriously hung up on someone who was, for all intents and purposes, the enemy. Humans and Vithii might've shared this colony planet successfully for almost a century before Temple had been born, but for as long as he could remember—the last twenty years, at least— the Vithii had been growing increasingly ethnocentric. It probably shouldn't have been as much of a surprise as it was when they eventually gained control of the government, and things erupted into full-blown fascism.

For most of his life, Temple had managed to fly under the radar. As a kid, he'd fallen in with the human gangs, taking odd jobs for them. With a sick mother and an absent father, the money he earned that way was often the difference between having enough food and going hungry. When his mom died and he was stuck into the foster care system, he'd cleaned up his act for a few years while he was living with his foster family. Once he was out on his own as an adult, though, he'd fallen back into the gray area populated by couriers and fixers who worked for the gangs. It was what he knew, after all, and it was a way to make the rent without getting involved directly in the really bad stuff—murder and extortion and drugs.

That worked fine, right up until the day he found out his foster father, Dr. Zarian Chantrell, had been blackmailed into creating a bioweapon that the Vithii Premiere intended to use against the humans in the Ilarian Capital. At which point, flying under the radar was no longer an option.

Against all odds, his sister Skye had managed to manufacture an antidote to the weapon and introduce it into the water supply in time to save a good chunk of the population. Temple acted as a decoy, drawing the guards' attention long enough to help her escape the Regime complex where their father was being held, after he slipped her the chemical formula for the antitoxin. Temple had paid for that 'decoy' stunt with his freedom, and if the higher-ups decided his usefulness wasn't worth the cost of his upkeep in prison, he might well end up paying for it with his life as well. Most days, he tried to convince himself that was a decent trade-off.

Some days, he even believed it.

So, yeah, maybe this Vithii doctor who wasn't actually a doctor had been kind to him… or at least professional toward him. Maybe she did have striking eyes and strong cheekbones, and red hair that seemed as angry and defiant as she was. Maybe she *was* built like an Amazon warrior, and—

He started to shake his head as if to clear it, but stopped himself just in time, not wanting to alarm the guards—or give them an excuse to beat the shit out of him while he was still carrying the mementoes of his *last* beating.

Fuck. How long had it actually been since he'd gotten laid?

Get a grip, shithead, he told himself sternly. *No obsessing over people who would very likely prefer to see your entire species wiped out. Especially ones who are in imminent danger of taking a dirt-nap in the unmarked grave right next door to yours.*

Fortunately, his cell was just ahead. His guards stopped him a few steps away, and the taller one entered the code to trigger the door. A rough hand in the center of his back shoved him inside, and he caught himself against the far wall with the skill of far too much practice. The door clanged shut behind him, leaving him once again in the blank box that was barely big enough to turn around in.

The rational part of his mind knew that he was safer in here than he would be most other places inside the prison. The less rational part—the part that had been staring at these grimy walls for the better part of a month now—felt the familiar wash of panic that was getting harder and harder to hold at bay.

How much longer would he be stuck in this place before they either killed his pathetic ass or revealed their plan to use him to somehow get to Skye? Was his foster sister still alive? He was beginning to think that she must be. Otherwise, he didn't see why they'd bother with him as much as they had been.

Sad to say, what he was getting these days was considered special treatment… for a human, at least. Medical care? Regular meals? Even the damned cell, which was at least private. Yeah—they needed him. He only hoped that he wouldn't come to regret all that 'special treatment,' once he found out what they needed him *for.*

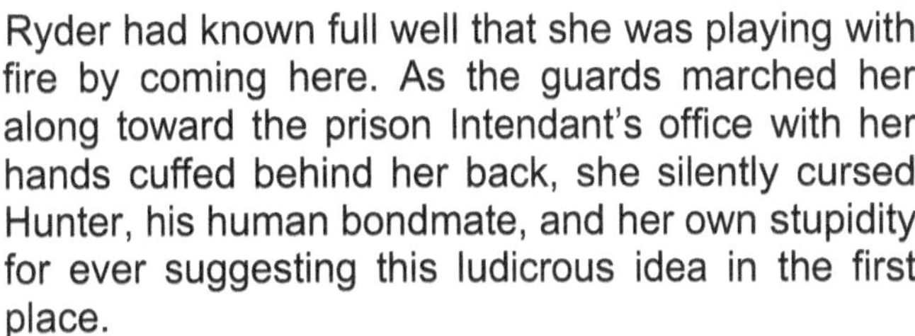

Ryder had known full well that she was playing with fire by coming here. As the guards marched her along toward the prison Intendant's office with her hands cuffed behind her back, she silently cursed Hunter, his human bondmate, and her own stupidity for ever suggesting this ludicrous idea in the first place.

When Ash discovered that Skye's foster brother had survived capture and was being held in a Regime prison, there was no question that they would attempt to get him out. Hunter had pledged protection of Skye's House during the pair's bonding ceremony, and, prophets help her, so had Ryder. She'd made a blood offering after the ceremony, right along with the rest of them. She was part of Hunter's House—for all practical purposes, at least.

She certainly didn't have any other House to call her own. Not since her bondmate had renounced her and made her *grei'kaapt.* Untouchable.

Like Kade, Draven, and all the others, she was House Shadow Wing now, and House Shadow Wing was under a blood vow to act in the best interest of House Chantrell 'for as long as the last member of each House shall live.' Which, at this rate, didn't look like it was going to be very *fucking* long.

Ryder had been the only one of them with a half-decent shot at getting in and getting access to the prisoner records—not to mention access to the prisoners themselves. Ash and Skye were human. Pax was a cyborg. Kade had been a prisoner here himself, and still bore the chronic neurotonin addiction to prove it, after the guards' attempts to keep him quiet and tractable using drugs. Hunter was far too recognizable with his distinctive feathered tattoos.

Draven had offered, and in hindsight, it was pretty clear she should have jumped on his suggestion. He might well have been able to infiltrate the place in a low-level menial job of some sort. But, no, of course she'd had to stick her neck into the noose, and point out that he would have a difficult time gaining access to sensitive information without risking exposure.

Much better to send in someone who could pose as a doctor, right? Yeah, because that had worked out *so* well. For someone who used to perform brain surgery for a living, Ryder was a bloody idiot.

She calmed her nerves by fantasizing about whose ass she would kick first—Hunter's or Ash's. Ridiculous as it was, she was still battling shock over the fact that her cover had been blown in the first place. Ash's identity documents had *never* let them down before—as evidenced by the fact that they were all still alive.

For the moment, at least.

Ash had walked her through the entire electronic and paper trail in detail before she'd gone in. She couldn't see any way that her real identity would have been revealed. Especially not so quickly—it had only been a few days, and the wheels of bureaucracy were notorious for their slow, ponderous method of grinding through data.

Does it really matter? she thought angrily.

But it did. If she had been compromised, there was a chance the others were in danger, too. She would need to try to find out what had happened, though the pessimistic part of her—which was a pretty fucking *large* part of her, these days—helpfully pointed out that there wouldn't be much she could do with the information from *inside the prison*.

If they had the kind of proof against her that would stand up in the Regime's bad joke of a court system, she was either going to end up dead, or rotting at the bottom of a hole so deep that she'd wish she was dead. It was no coincidence that the snot-nosed guard who'd burst into the infirmary just as she was about to convey a message to Skye's brother had made a point of specifying *capital crimes*. They wanted Ryder afraid, and they wanted her off balance.

It was working, though she would rather saw off her right hand with a rusty scalpel than let them see it.

The Intendant's office was clean and cheery—a sick joke inside a place like this. A chirpy human woman sat at a desk in the reception area, wearing a frilly blouse that displayed an unnecessary amount of cleavage. Ryder wanted to sneer at her. Where did the Regime find these humans who seemed willing to turn a blind eye to the inconvenient fact that their employers wanted to commit genocide against their own species?

The answer was obvious, though. The humans who assisted the Regime did so in hopes that they and their loved ones would be spared if they scraped in the dirt at the Premiere's feet and offered to lick his boots clean. Were they right? Ryder prayed none of them ever had to find out.

"May I help you?" the girl asked in a too-sweet voice.

"Prisoner Erisuel to see the Intendant," the senior guard snapped, "on his orders."

The receptionist smiled at him with blank eyes and tapped the edge of her heads-up display. Her gaze flickered over the data feed for a moment before she looked at them again and said, "Go on through. He's expecting you."

Already, it was clear this was no ordinary arrest. No way did the Intendant have prisoners paraded through his shiny office on a regular basis so he could speak with them personally. Ryder's pulse quickened as a flush of foreboding went through her, and she gritted her teeth. She would *not* give these people the satisfaction of seeing her afraid.

If they knew her name, they already considered her no better than dirt beneath their feet. She would fucking well stand there and look the Intendant in the eye without backing down, just as she'd done to every other piece of garbage who'd dared judge her on the basis of either biology or philosophical conviction. Ryder had done plenty of things over the years that could be judged. But she wasn't giving them this one.

The door to the Intendant's inner sanctum whooshed open smoothly, a breath of perfumed air wafting out as it did.

"Come in," said the man who held the lives of more than a thousand prisoners, human and Vithii, under his control.

He was hard. Grizzled. His rough presence did not sit well inside this airy corner office with its expensive art and the scent of *trinah* blossoms floating in the air from an electronically controlled dispenser. Ryder's eyes flicked to a second figure standing in the corner—a figure that seemed far more diffident and uncomfortable than the man sitting behind the large, *chik'taap*-wood desk. A figure that was oddly familiar.

"So," said the Intendant, turning to the second man, "you're certain it's her?"

The Vithii in the corner moved forward, his spine bent in a submissive slouch as he peered across the room at Ryder. With a jolt, she recognized one of the orderlies from the hospital where she had worked years ago. Before—

"Yeah," said the man. Ryder couldn't even remember his name after all this time. "She dyed her hair and changed her eye color, but that's definitely her. That's Dr. Erisuel."

TWO

For about the dozenth time in the last few minutes, Ryder cursed herself for her stupidity. After so many years spent trying to be invisible, it hadn't occurred to her that she might stumble on someone who'd known her in the time *before*. The time when she'd been a respected surgeon, minding her own business and pursuing a promising career.

In many ways, it felt like an entirely different lifetime. How could anyone possibly recognize the person she'd been then by looking at the person she was now? Not just because of the red hair or the brown eyes, but also because she wasn't remotely the same woman she'd been eight years ago.

"I have no idea who this person is," she said, refusing to show any outward reaction. "I also have no idea who this Erisuel person is supposed to be. I'm Dr. Elspen Radathian. Which, frankly, you should already know since you hired me barely two weeks ago. I demand that you release me immediately so I can get back to my patients—though I feel I should make it clear that I'll be tendering my two weeks' notice of resignation just as soon as I can get to a terminal."

The Intendant released a huff of air that might have been interpreted as amusement.

"I believe we can take your immediate termination of employment as read," he said, eyeing her like she was a mildly interesting microbe under the lens of a microscope. "You will relinquish a DNA sample for comparative analysis with records on file, and if, as I suspect, your DNA is a match, then you will not be accessing any terminals for the foreseeable future, child-killer."

All of Ryder's carefully planned legal arguments for why she would sure as fuck *not* be relinquishing a DNA sample fell away at the same time her stomach did. The lurch of nausea at the sudden reminder of the worst day of her life nearly made her knees buckle, and it was all she could do to lock her legs in place and keep her eyes from squeezing shut in remembered agony. Any arguments were rendered moot a moment later, when one of the guards plucked a few strands of hair from her scalp.

She hadn't even seen him move.

"This is a mistake," she said hoarsely.

The Intendant tilted his head, regarding her with interest. "It was certainly a mistake on your part. It's not often that a criminal as notorious as Aryderlyn Erisuel voluntarily walks into a prison and requests a job. It makes me wonder what other conspiracies are at play, here."

Ryder pressed her lips together and remained silent.

He continued to pin her with sharp blue eyes for another long moment, before he shrugged and moved his attention to a file on his desk. "Still, I suppose that sort of thing isn't really within my remit. Once the sample is run and your identity is confirmed, I will contact the Under-Minister of Military Logistics and inform him that you are in custody."

Ryder's blood ran cold.

The Intendant's eyes flicked up to her again, and he lifted a heavy brow. "I'm certain that your bondmate will be… quite interested in discovering what you've been up to since you escaped justice for your crimes."

Ryder's awareness stuttered in fits and starts as the guards marched her out of the Intendant's office, through the warren of prison tunnels to the processing area. She tried to tell herself that there was still time for the others to figure out something had gone wrong and come up with a plan. It would take a day or so to run the DNA and compare the results to her file.

Then, if Jodor—

Her brain stumbled over the name, and her feet nearly stumbled over nothing at the same time. She steeled herself. If Jodor Erisuel—her bondmate—was coming, it would take additional time for him to get the message and arrive here.

And she really needed not to think about him right now, because she was shortly going to have more immediate things to worry about. The others would figure out she was compromised, and somehow they'd get to her in time. End of story.

Optimism doesn't suit you, whispered an unwelcome voice in the back of her head.

Neither does blind panic, she shot back.

So. Prisoner processing.

She gathered it was different depending on whether a prisoner was human or Vithii, and whether they had any perceived political value or not. Did she have any perceived political value? That was an interesting question… or it would have been an interesting question if there weren't so much weight riding on the answer.

Ryder was of interest to one mid-level Regime official in particular—that much was certain. She was also an embarrassment and a scandal to the aforementioned mid-level Regime official. That same mid-level Regime official had additionally tried to have her killed eight years ago, to cover up said scandal. Unfortunately, Ryder had never understood politics even back when she was bonded to a politician, so she had no idea if that qualified as political value.

The guards dragged her to an automated tattoo station and forced her arm into the slot at the front of the machine, withdrawing it several painful moments later to reveal the black barcode inked into the flesh of her forearm. At that point, she decided it probably didn't qualify. When they marched her into a bare room with the one-way mirror on the wall and ordered her to strip, she was sure.

She crammed her anger and humiliation down deep, knowing more or less how this was likely to play out.

"You'll probably want to get female guards for this," she suggested.

The senior guard leered, his earlier professionalism evaporating like mist now that he'd done his duty and paraded her in front of the Intendant like a good little soldier. "Nah, Red. We're good like this. You wouldn't want to get written up for insubordination to a guard on your very first day in the slammer, would you?" he asked, his teeth bared in a grin.

The other guard nearly wheezed in amusement. "We just want to see for ourselves whether the rumors are true, pet."

Ryder shrugged and let them un-cuff her hands. She started efficiently stripping off her lab coat and scrubs, feigning indifference even as her blood ran hot with a combination of rage and shame. Rage *at* the shame, which she could no more control than she could control her involuntary nervous system.

Or her fucking endocrine system, more to the point.

The sordid and predictable script played out as she had known it would. As more and more of her skin was revealed to the mouth-breathers watching her avidly, the air in the stuffy room grew musky with their burgeoning arousal. She breathed it in, the pheromones hitting receptors inside her nasal passages and on the back of her tongue. Normally, when the receptors of a bonded female were activated, they would send a signal to the gland at the juncture of her neck and shoulder. That gland would start pumping out a different sort of pheromone—one combining the scent of both the female and the male she was bonded to.

Other males reacted instinctively to that scent, which killed sexual arousal, generating feelings of protectiveness and respect instead. An elegant evolutionary solution to minimize conflict in an aggressive species that mated for life, she'd always thought… right up until she'd learned first-hand about the cruel joke hidden under the elegance.

Because while a mating bond might be lifelong, Vithii—like other species—had free will. They could leave. They could betray. They could come to hate that which they had once loved, or at least, that which they had once desired.

A mated Vithii female could never turn back the clock and become un-mated, but without regular sexual contact during which the male's saliva stimulated the female's gland with a mating bite, the pheromone she produced would scream to every male within scenting distance that her mate had abandoned her, and left her *grei'kaapt*.

As Jodor Erisuel had left Ryder *grei'kaapt,* some eight years ago now.

It wasn't so bad for those females past the age of childbearing—those who had lost their mates to death. Merely a vague feeling of unpleasantness that was generally recognized for what it was and politely ignored. But for Vithii women in their prime, who had been abandoned either through choice or untimely death? The pheromone that should have engendered positive feelings from unfamiliar, un-bonded males incited feelings of anger and disgust instead.

A natural evolutionary step allowing males to identify females who might be undesirable breeders, for whatever reason, one of Ryder's male professors in medical school had opined in a blithe tone. *Unfortunate, but understandable.*

Many females, he'd gone on to explain in serious tones, went so far as to have the entire mating gland surgically removed after losing their mates, despite the societal disapproval for such an extreme reaction to a natural process.

At the time, Ryder had rolled her eyes and dutifully taken notes, drawing a stupid little frowny face with its tongue sticking out next to the notation. Six years later, she'd learned what it meant to be untouchable—an outcast. And she'd lived that way ever since.

As a fugitive, she wasn't really in a position to explore the surgical option. While she might have found a back alley practitioner somewhere who would be willing to do it, the procedure would leave her sick and weak for some time afterward as her body recovered from the blow to a vital physical system. Maybe she could have gotten away with it after she'd hooked up with Hunter and the others, but even with other people available to help, her life was not what one would call relaxed.

So, with the two guards gaping at her like she was some sort of exotic prostitute rather than a thirty-eight-year-old former doctor, her body started its involuntary efforts to defuse the situation, and ended up doing exactly the opposite.

Fucking evolution.

The mouthy one barged into her personal space and put a hand on her, only to jerk it back as though she'd burned him, rubbing his fingers together like she'd dirtied him somehow.

"What the fuck is that shit?" he sneered. "Guess they were right about you, bitch. That is *foul*."

Both guards crowded in, simultaneously fascinated and repulsed.

"Ugh," said the second one. "No way am I putting my hands all over that."

They were so distracted by her pheromones that she honestly thought she might have been able to overpower them. It was deeply, dangerously tempting. If she could get one of their sidearms...

She shook her head. If she could get a sidearm, then what? She was on the wrong side of the prison walls, and every scan point she passed would pick up the barcode freshly tattooed into her forearm like it was a beacon. She was surrounded by guards, checkpoints, and automatic weapons arrays.

"I told you that you should get female guards for this," she said in a flat tone, still pushing down all the things that wanted to explode outward in an eruption of violence, frustration, and self-loathing. She realized that she was physically trembling with the effort required to hold it all inside.

The moment of pregnant possibility passed as the first guard seemed to remember himself and pulled his sidearm, using the blunt muzzle to shove her backward.

"Up against the wall and stay there, *grei'kaapt.* Zan, comm someone from the women's side to get over here and take her. We don't get paid enough to touch that kind of filth."

Ryder raised an eyebrow, playing at being un-affected. "If you'd stuck to thinking with your brains instead of thinking with your dicks, we could have had a nice little interlude and been on our merry ways."

The guard's expression might have been the same shape as a smile, but that's where the simi-larity ended. "*Nice.* No surprise that your mate dropped you like a contagious disease. I'm guess-ing since that part's true, the rest of it is as well. Is that right, baby killer?"

Ryder was silent, and the man let out a grating laugh.

Zan retreated to the door, obviously eager for the relief guards to show up. Fortunately for every-one, they didn't have too long to wait, and Ryder was summarily handed over to two towering, heavy-set Vithii women wearing the same severe uniforms and sidearms as the first pair.

The strip search was completed with the requisite amount of awkwardness and humiliation. At least the newcomers both appeared to be women of few words. After they were done, Ryder was presented with one of the shapeless smocks all the female Vithii prisoners wore. One of the guards cuffed her hands again, and she was herded off to the confinement level.

Any hope she might have held out that she would get special treatment disappeared when they arrived at a filthy communal cell containing about two dozen female prisoners—all Vithii. Without a word, the taller of the guards gestured the inmates back from the door with her weapon, and the shorter one—who still had a full head of height over Ryder—shoved her inside. The heavy door slammed closed behind her.

She turned slowly, taking stock of the figures arrayed around the echoing space. She knew this might well be the point where the violence she'd held back earlier would be the only thing to keep her alive. Not everyone here was a threat, but several of them almost certainly were. She had no possessions except the ugly gray smock, but the dangerous ones still might find value in beating the crap out of her to keep the rest of their cellmates cowed. One of the women sniffed the air.

"What's that stench?" she asked. "Why the fuck are you in here stinking up the place, bitch?"

Ryder said nothing, weighing the speaker's potential as an opponent. She was confident she could take the woman down unless she was hiding a shiv like the one that had slashed Skye's brother… or unless the others piled in and overwhelmed her with numbers.

"You got a tongue?" the woman prodded.

"I have a tongue," Ryder said cautiously.

One of the others she had pegged as being among the alphas of the group tilted her head curiously upon hearing her voice. She looked familiar, Ryder realized, having been less attentive to specific faces earlier than she'd been to body language and demeanor.

"You," Ryder said. "You were in the infirmary for an infection two days ago."

The woman blinked, clearly surprised. "I thought I recognized you. You're that new doctor. What in the prophets' names are you doing down here in the pit?"

Ryder took a breath, softening her body language incrementally, and gestured at her smock. "Being imprisoned, apparently."

"What for?" asked the woman.

"Case of mistaken identity," Ryder said dismissively, and changed the subject. "How's that wound doing? Do you want me to take another look at it?"

The woman pulled the edge of her stained smock up and peered around at her hip. "Oh. You know—it's a bit better now. It stopped weeping and I think it's closing over."

Ryder nodded, and cautiously made her way through the other prisoners until she got to her former patient. The wound would have benefited from a stent for drainage, but it appeared to finally be healing properly as she had said.

"That looks good," she said. "I'm glad."

The woman smiled, revealing gaps in her teeth. She jerked her chin toward a thin woman with gaunt features who was huddled in the corner. "That one's sick. Throws up everything she tries to eat. You should take a look at her."

Ryder nodded agreeably, feeling the atmosphere shifting around her to something less loaded. "Sure thing." The sick woman looked up at her mistrustfully, but answered Ryder's simple questions and submitted to a hand on her brow to check for fever.

"Probably enteritis from bacteria in the food or water," she diagnosed. "Have you tried to go to the infirmary?"

The woman nodded, and her neighbor said, "They wouldn't let her."

"Hmm," Ryder said. "In the morning, pretend to be sicker than you are and see if you can get them to take you. If not, the best thing to try is fasting completely for a full day and night. It might give your gut a chance to recover a bit."

A couple more of the women offered up physical complaints, and Ryder played doctor as much as possible with no equipment, supplies, or medicine available. By the time she was done, the restless energy of potential violence had quieted back to apathy. She staked out a stretch of grimy wall to lean against as the others settled for the night.

Ryder wasn't about to sleep—a tentative truce did not equal safety. But, as the night wore on, she leaned her head back and let her eyes slip closed as she listened to the snores and coughs coming from the other prisoners. Toward morning, her mind started to drift despite her best efforts, floating back to hazy images caught somewhere between dream and memory. Images of a night far worse than even this one.

The night her bondmate had tried to have her killed.

THREE

Ash tapped his fingers rhythmically against the desktop as he stared at the flashing time readout displayed on the chrono. There was nothing for it—Ryder should have checked in by now unless something had happened to prevent her, without question. She knew perfectly well how vital her nightly check-in was, and she was too much of a professional to blow it off.

Something was wrong.

There were three main possibilities. One—Ryder was injured and unable to reach a comm unit. Two—Ryder had been captured. Three—Ryder was dead. Ash wondered when, exactly, he'd reached this uncomfortable point in his existence where 'because they're dead' was automatically part of the shortlist of explanations for anything unusual involving the handful of people he actually gave a damn about.

The slow-burning bitterness that seemed as much a part of his existence these days as eating or taking a shower rose up, demanding attention. It was a good thing he had so much practice ignoring it, he supposed, since emotions were a waste of time that Ryder couldn't afford right now. He flicked the switch on the transmitter, waiting about forty-five seconds until the automatic government security sweep completed a full scan of the useable frequencies before examining the results with a critical eye.

Hoping that whoever was on the other end of the transmission hadn't dozed off at the comms, he sent a quick burst along a double-sideband suppressed-carrier frequency, containing the coded decryption information for the main message. After giving the recipient another sixty seconds to implement the decryption, he opened the main communication line and turned on the mic.

The transmission would swap frequencies every few seconds, running ahead of the government's pattern of sweeping through the carrier bands without ever letting the scan catch up... unless the Regime snoops changed that pattern at an unexpected moment.

The whole thing was a bloody pain in Ash's backside. Still, two of their seven safe houses had already been raided in the weeks since the Premiere had tried to unleash a bioweapon on the humans in the Capital. Even with Kade's deep pockets to fund them, they couldn't really afford to keep losing boltholes at that rate. They needed to stay untraceable.

Confirming that his transmission was flying successfully under the radar, Ash spoke into the mic.

"Get everyone to Location Four right away," he said grimly. "We have a problem."

———◆———

Less than two cycles later, the room full of cobbled-together tech was jammed with four hulking Vithii, plus Skye and Ash. Skye was pacing, the others trying to give her space until Hunter gently caught her by the shoulders, stilling her. She crossed her arms, tension vibrating around her body like a cloud, her twitchiness not doing much for Ash's nerves, either.

"This is my fault," she said in a tight voice. "It was too dangerous. I should never have let her go."

"She volunteered," Pax replied. The cyborg's voice was as flat and emotionless as ever. "Hindsight and second-guessing are not valuable. Strategy is."

Skye glared at him, so different now from the terrified human civvy who'd nearly fainted on the spot upon realizing that she was in the same room with a Vithii military cyborg.

"She's your friend, too, Pax!"

Pax raised an eyebrow, the movement making light shift across the silver filigree embedded in the side of his face. "Yes. She is. Hence the need for devising strategy to get her back."

Skye glared at him for another few seconds before she sagged a bit in Hunter's grip, raising a hand to scrub across her face. "So what do we do?"

Draven shifted. "I could still go in after her."

Ash knew that his negative gut reaction to that idea was irrational. It also irritated the hell out of him. Somehow, neither of those things kept him from saying, "No. Not until we know more about what happened."

Draven's disconcerting golden gaze landed on him in a way that made the latest round of raw skin and bruises on Ash's back itch uncomfortably, but he was damned if he'd let it show. He narrowed his eyes and held Draven's stare, feeling his face harden into a frown.

Hunter broke the small standoff. "Is there another way to find out what happened without getting eyes inside?"

Ash tore his eyes away from Draven to answer him. "Possibly. The prison's computers are locked down pretty tight. But the vulnerability I exploited in the first place, when I was able to confirm that Temple was alive and being held, still hasn't been patched. I can't access prisoner records directly, but if any messages about Ryder are sent to other government agencies through the unsecured server, I can flag them based on keywords."

He frowned, as something… rather important occurred to him. "Or at least I can if the messages mention her fake identity. Does anyone here even know her real name?"

How odd that he'd never thought to ask her before. Ash supposed such things came with the territory of being criminals and fugitives, but even so—

"Her name was Aryderlyn Erisuel," Pax said, "and even if it ends up saving her life, she will not thank me for telling you."

Kade grunted dismissively. "Since 'pissed off' is her default mood setting, I doubt we'll even notice," he added, not moving from his position propping up the wall next to the doorway.

"She doesn't have to be happy about it," Skye said, still looking lost. "She just has to come back safe."

In the part of his psyche that wasn't packed up tight and emotionless, Ash felt for Skye. She'd been presented with the choice of risking her friend's life or letting her brother rot in a Vithii prison. Ash had known as soon as he'd dug up confirmation of

Temple's arrest and detainment that relaying the information to the others would further complicate their already very complicated lives.

Ignoring things like that wasn't who they were, though. Even if Hunter hadn't tied them all to Skye's family by bonding with her, it would have been a betrayal of what they stood for to turn their backs on the man. Temple Akenzua had played a key role in saving the humans in the Capital from death at the hands of the Premiere's bioweapon. They weren't about to let him languish in the Regime's hellhole of a prison system if they could do something about it.

Ash glanced at Hunter. "Let me have until mid-morning tomorrow before you risk anyone else on direct reconnaissance. I'll get you a report by ten-hundred hours."

Hunter nodded. "Very well, *leetha*. We will wait until then."

Ash took a centering breath. "Right. In that case… bugger off, you lot, and let me work." He didn't wait, but turned immediately back to the mass of screens and keyboards piled haphazardly on the desk. A furrow formed between his brows. "*Aryderlyn Erisuel*. How strange. That name really doesn't suit her at all."

◆

Hours later, Ash yawned and stretched. His spine ached, and he winced as his back reminded him helpfully of the latest round of abuse it had received at the hands of a certain minor official with loose lips and an unhealthy appetite for things that would eventually get him into trouble. He put those thoughts aside with the ease of long practice, unwilling to dwell on them when there was more important work to do.

The insecure server was indeed still insecure, and all messages going through it would now be scanned for any reference to 'Radathian,' 'Erisuel,' 'Aryderlyn,' or 'Doctor.' With the surveillance program in place and running smoothly, Ash turned his attention to other matters. He'd debated with himself for some time before deciding that he valued Ryder's life more than he valued her privacy. He was willing to risk her ire if it meant possibly uncovering information that could help them get her back.

Opening up a browser window, he applied the many layers of protection and encryption that would prevent anyone in the government from tracking the search activity back to a server or IP address. A quarter-cycle later, he pushed back from the desk, slouching into his battered chair. The half-healed whip marks on his back screamed a protest, but he barely noticed as he stared at the collection of news releases and court documents scattered across his screens.

"Son of a *bitch*, Ryder," he murmured. "Why didn't you ever tell us?"

***

In Ryder's dream, she was younger and less steeped in the world's cruelty. Not *young*, certainly—but not the bitter, closed-off thing she would eventually become. Had she been a better person eight years ago, when the vicious unfairness of fate's whimsy had still taken her by surprise? When it had still sliced through her like an unexpected knife in the gut?

No. Perhaps she hadn't been. Eight years ago, she had already made the choice that would condemn her forever. She just hadn't felt the full bite of the repercussions yet.

She remembered the shock of grief and self-doubt. The realization that what had seemed so right and obvious and necessary at the time might well have been the worst thing she could possibly have done.

She remembered her growing desperation as Jodor pulled away from her. She could picture every nuance in the way his expression grew cold and hard as she explained what she had done and why. Even as she'd done it, she'd known it was illegal. She wasn't an idiot. *Of course* it was illegal. But just because something was against the law didn't mean it was automatically wrong in a moral sense.

Ryder had been living the life of her dreams. Real human fairy tale stuff—an amazing career in a respected medical field. A rich husband making his way up the political ranks in the new government party. A beautiful baby boy—the first, she hoped, of many.

Looking back, she could see the hairline cracks in the facade of perfection. She could see the hints of what the new political party would become, with its charismatic leader subtly blending Vithii populism with underlying Vithii xenophobia. But she hadn't been worried about the humans and their rights, back then. Why should she be? The humans were fine. If anything, it was Vithii who had always been at a disadvantage since their refugee ships had arrived on the fledgling human colony planet some hundred years before.

With hindsight, she could also see the tiny cracks in her relationship with her bondmate. The way he was more invested in her appearance and her career than in her as a person. The way his affection and attention hinged on how well she was meeting his demands at any given moment.

She was what the humans labeled 'arm-candy,' a term that had angered her considerably the first time someone explained it to her. *The truth hurts…* another human phrase that often hit far too close to home for comfort. Still, it was easy enough to ignore the little niggling doubts. No bonding was perfect, but they were *Vithii*. Vithii mated for life.

Humans who dared to comment had no idea how ironic they were being. As if Ryder was interested in hearing relationship advice from a species that married and divorced and remarried as if it were all a great big game to them—*what nerve*. She and Jodor would be fine because they were bondmates, and bondmates were always fine.

Right up until the horrible day when they weren't.

The grief that day had been more crippling than anything she had ever experienced in her life. She'd needed Jodor—needed him so badly. She told herself that maybe together, the two of them could hold each other's broken pieces together until the sharp edges started to mend. Instead of comfort, though, she'd encountered anger. Rage.

Rage directed squarely at *her*.

"You're supposed to be a doctor!" he'd snarled at her. "You should have thought of something better than this!"

She staggered back a step, stunned. "I tried *everything*, Jodor! I nearly killed myself developing new things to try! *Do you think I wanted this to happen*?"

If his anger had shocked her, his next words chilled her to the bone.

"You've ruined me," he said, his voice grown cold. "My family... my career. Get out of my sight, you useless, evil creature. You are no longer welcome in my house."

Ryder couldn't remember leaving the house. Indeed, her next clear memory was of sitting on a chair in a darkened hotel room, staring at the screen of her personal comm device. There were half a dozen messages from her supervisor at the hospital where she'd worked, each one worded increasingly strongly, demanding an immediate response, until the last one terminating her employment and advising her that certain matters relating to her recent medical conduct had been turned over to law enforcement.

There were no messages from either her bondmate or her family. She knew with sick certainty that Jodor had already gotten to them and told them what she had done. That had been the real moment when everything had come crashing down around her, as she truly understood for the first time what her actions had wrought.

For more than a week, she hid out in that awful hotel room with its beige walls and hideous, mass-produced art. Her mind was muddled by grief, fear, and depression—but even so, as a doctor she recognized the beginning stages of bonding withdrawal. Without regular contact with her mate, her body was changing, and she hated the feeling with every fiber of her being. Instinct screamed that she was upset, she was in danger, and her mate should be *here*, protecting her. Comforting her. But instead, he had abandoned her.

Two days later, her credit chip was declined by the hotel's payment system. Perhaps Jodor had restricted access to her account in some way, or perhaps law enforcement had done it. Either way, she was now unable to pay for the room. Her mind was not working rationally by that point, but something warned her to stay away from family members or acquaintances, in case the authorities were watching them in hopes she would contact them.

As she sat later that night in a deserted café, sipping *edelveen* that she'd purchased with the last of her cash to keep the staff from throwing her out, her comm unit buzzed. She nearly pounced on it, desperate for any kind of news… any kind of inter-action. Her heart raced as she recognized Jodor's private comm code—the one he used for confiden-tial business.

Meet me in the alley behind the Consigliere Club at oh-one-hundred. We need to talk.

Thumbs flying, she typed out a return message asking what was going on and if he'd had anything to do with her credit account being blocked. There was no reply, nor were there any replies to the next eight messages she sent him. With nothing else to do, she tapped her foot restlessly against the faded tile floor of the café until the awkward, pimply hu-man behind the counter finally asked her to leave so he could close up.

Then, she made her way slowly toward the *Consigliere* on foot, dragging her single, sad suit-case behind her. She was slightly familiar with the place. It was a high-end club for professionals, mostly Vithii, though not exclusively. She'd been there… twice, maybe? Both times had been shortly after her graduation from medical school, when her new colleagues from her residency position had dragged her out for 'networking.'

She'd learned quickly that networking was code for getting drunk or high and then trying to hook up for casual sex. Since none of those things particularly appealed to her, she'd found excuses to beg off after the first couple of times.

The tiny corner of her brain that was trying to keep a handle on rationality pointed out that it seemed an odd choice of venue on Jodor's part. The place wasn't a hangout for political types, unless it had changed in recent years. Certainly, Jodor had never mentioned going there before.

Maybe he was worried that he was being watched, she thought.

She cooled her heels across the street for the last half-hour before they were due to meet, fantasizing about the way he'd forgive her and apologize for behaving the way he had. He would take her in his arms, nipping at the skin over her mating gland and easing the horrible ache that had taken up residence there over the course of the last week.

And everything would be fine.

Her comm alarm buzzed, letting her know it was oh-one-hundred. She frowned. She'd chosen this spot so she'd have a clear view of him arriving. Was he late? Or had she been too wrapped up in her daydreams and missed seeing him?

Nervously, she crossed the nearly deserted street and headed into the alley used for deliveries to the club. It was about an hour before closing time; not many people were out. "Hello?" she called, trying to peer into the shadows.

A moment later, Jodor appeared in a shaft of light filtering in from the roof of a nearby building. "Hello, Lyn," he said, using his nickname for her. "You've caused me quite a number of problems, you know."

She didn't even think, she just followed the pull of the mating bond and rushed toward him, the squeaky wheels of the little suitcase jerking and jumping against the grit of the alley floor.

"Jodor!" she exclaimed, needing to feel him against her *right now*. She gasped as large hands closed around her arms from either side, jerking her to a halt. "What—? Jodor, *what's going on*?"

The two brawny Vithii men—both complete strangers—tightened their grip as she tried to jerk free.

"I told you," Jodor said. "You're causing problems. Minister Kovak made it clear that I needed to make those problems go away if I wanted to maintain my position in the Vithii First movement. So that's what I'm doing."

The men holding her dragged her forward until she was standing in the patch of pale sodium light filtering down from above. The one on her right lifted a compact laser blaster in one hand, its snub nose made of a dark synthetic material that seemed to swallow the weak yellow light. Her eyes widened, breath catching in her throat. As a doctor, she'd seen what those sleek little weapons could do to a person's body.

"You obviously had a breakdown of some sort," Jodor continued in a tone of regret. "So sad that you ran off on your own and committed suicide in a back alley rather than turn yourself over to the justice system."

She tried to swallow against the dryness in her throat and choked. "You wouldn't," she whispered.

"Of course not," he said. "As far as the authorities will be concerned, I had nothing to do with it. Still… it's far less of a scandal this way. Much better than a lengthy trial would be." His eyes moved to the man on her right. "Wait until I'm gone, and do it quickly. Make sure to get her fingerprints on the weapon."

With that, Jodor turned and walked out of her life, leaving her standing between a pair of hired killers.

When he was gone, the man with the blaster moved in front of her and looked down. "Right, girlie. Don't struggle, and I promise you won't feel a thing."

He raised the weapon and without even thinking, she jammed her knee into his groin with every bit of strength she possessed. Rage flooded through her as he doubled over in surprise, and she grabbed the stubby barrel of the blaster. It went off, the heat burning her palm and scorching past her left shoulder, so close she thought it might have left a blackened patch on her shirtsleeve. The second thug choked on a cry and collapsed, a smoking hole through his chest.

Fueled by panic and fury, she wrenched the weapon in the other direction and the man lost his grip, stumbling back. Disgusted, she dropped the gun at her feet and grabbed the handle of her rolling suitcase in both hands, swinging the heavy end at his head. He dropped like a stone and didn't move.

Running on autopilot, she crouched and checked his pulse, feeling its steady thrum, hearing the rasp of his breathing. There was nothing to be done for the other one. Her eyes fell on the blaster discarded on the ground an arm's length away. She stared at it for a long moment, her hand hovering a hairsbreadth above the still-warm weapon. Eventually, her fingers closed around it and she shoved it in her trouser pocket. Grabbing her suitcase—now slightly dented—she hurried out of the alley. She didn't look back at the unconscious Vithii male, or at the dead body beside him.

It was the body of either the first person she'd ever killed, or the second… depending on whom you asked.

FOUR

"Prisoner two-four-one-three-nine, face the back wall and present your hands to be manacled!" barked a harsh Vithii voice.

Temple blinked awake, startled from sleep. As it did every morning after he'd been able to manage more than a light doze, the brief moment of disorientation gave way to a familiar sinking feeling as reality reasserted itself. He had been captured. He was in a Regime prison. He didn't know if his foster father and sister were dead or alive.

Knowing that any delay would come back to haunt him sooner rather than later, Temple scrambled to his feet in the cramped space, grunting as the slice across his chest made itself known. He glanced down at it as he shuffled around to stick his wrists through the gap in the cell bars so the guards could snap on a set of cuffs. The wound was no longer bleeding, praise the gods and prophets, but it pulled painfully as the guard outside jerked his wrists closer together.

Charming.

"Step forward!"

Temple didn't recognize this particular guard's voice, but he certainly seemed... enthusiastic about things. He did as he was bid and the cell door creaked open. Meaty hands grabbed his arms and hauled him backward, holding him while a second guard fitted the so-called *muzzle*—a metal gag that held the jaw wide open and strapped around the head, preventing clear speech.

Temple fucking hated the goddamned thing. Not only was it uncomfortable and humiliating, causing uncontrolled drooling after only a minute or two of use—it was also so disgustingly unhygienic that if he thought about it too closely he was afraid he'd puke. Allegedly, it was only for inmates who were considered particularly dangerous. But, interestingly enough, he'd never seen a Vithii prisoner wearing one.

Or perhaps it wasn't very interesting. No one here was making any bones about the fact that humans were only sharing the prison's air with the high and mighty Vithii because the Premiere didn't have any better place to put them.

Except in the ground, he thought bitterly.

"Time for your morning exercise session, prisoner!" said the irritatingly enthusiastic guard. The second guard grumbled, apparently just about as happy as Temple was to be dealing with that kind of cheerfulness first thing in the morning. Which was to say, not happy at all.

Exercise session. Terrific. After the beating—and shivving—he'd taken two days ago, he'd hoped they'd give him a break for a bit. Especially after they'd hauled the prison doctor off in handcuffs before she could finish treating his knife wound. He spared a moment to wonder how she was faring as the first string of drool trickled down his chin and his jaw started to ache.

He would probably never find out. It wasn't as though human prisoners got a news digest every morning. And while there was such a thing as a grapevine even in a place like this, Temple knew nothing about the Vithii woman beyond her name.

It would be smarter to save his worry for himself, as he was led off to the latest round of abuse masquerading as entertainment for the guards. 'Exercise' was code for any situation the guards could dream up to incite a brawl between prisoners when the supervisors weren't around. He'd heard that betting was rife, with some of the prison employees lining their own pockets by acting as bookies. Color Temple… not all that shocked, to be honest.

Sometimes, the guards would throw gangs of Vithii and humans in the yard together, but the favorite scenario seemed to be putting a lone prisoner in with a group of hostile prisoners and betting on how many he could take down before he was overpowered. When Temple's turn had come two days previously, he'd managed to put three of them on the ground before one of his Vithii opponents pulled the shiv and ended things prematurely.

He hoped a bunch of the fuckers betting against him had lost money.

Temple supposed he had been lucky. He'd heard plenty of stories of humans getting killed that way, but apparently he was still considered too valuable for that. Though it did make him wonder why he was being tossed back into the shark tank while he was still wounded, if that was the case.

Behind him, the cheerful guard started flapping his mouth again, and Temple made himself tune into the blabber on the off chance that he might learn something valuable.

"This oughta be good," the guard was saying. "Lozzie told me that one of the sub-intendants told *her* there's a guy in the government who wants this *grei'kaapt* bitch to disappear before her case ends up in the court system. I don't know who she pissed off, but it sounds like she won't be around long."

That was the second time someone had mentioned that term recently. *Grei'kaapt.* Something like a Vithii divorcée, he was pretty sure. Was the butt of this morning's entertainment to be a Vithii woman? And if so, why were they dragging *him* to the yard?

The second guard grunted. "This one'll be a good addition, then. He took out three male Vithii before the rest brought him down a couple of days ago." A hand jabbed Temple between the shoulder blades, and he stumbled forward before righting himself. "I lost twenty credits on the fuckin' filth."

Well, that was one question answered. His mood lightened momentarily at the thought of Grumpy losing twenty cred, before souring again. He still had no real idea of what he'd be facing this morning in the so-called exercise yard, but it was pretty clear it wouldn't be pretty. Temple didn't mind bashing heads occasionally, at least in self-defense. Though, mind you, he'd prefer not to do it while sporting a knife wound that had barely closed over.

He also had no desire whatsoever to take part in anything a bunch of desperate human inmates were likely to do to a lone woman—even if she was Vithii scum.

⟨◆⟩

Ryder jerked back to awareness from the dream memory. The drab walls of the communal prison cell greeted her. Around her, most of the other inmates slept on. She hadn't meant to lose track of her surroundings like that, but she appeared to have gotten away with it. No one had bothered her, or even approached her as she dozed.

The murky overhead strip lighting was no different now than it ever was inside the prison, but the distant clanging of doors opening and shutting made her think it was probably morning. With luck, Ash would have realized she'd been compromised and contacted the others to begin planning… what?

She shook her head at herself, irritated. It wasn't as though six people were going to storm the place with blasters firing and stage a rescue operation. That was why she was here in the first place—reconnaissance so they could figure out a possible next step toward retrieving Skye's brother. Unfortunately, even though it had only been four days, Ryder's general impression of this place was that Skye's brother was pretty much fucked.

And so, now, was she.

Hunter wasn't dumb enough to keep sending in people one at a time so they could get nabbed like she had been. At least, she *hoped* he wasn't that dumb. He was prone to a surprising turn of sentimentality at times; one that had grown more noticeable since he'd bonded with a human woman. Still, Kade wouldn't let him do anything too monumentally stupid… probably.

Her musings were interrupted by the arrival of the guards. One of them rapped the end of a shock wand against the bars and barked, "Prisoner two-four-eight-one-seven! Come forward immediately!"

Ryder glanced around, noticing that no one seemed to be moving.

"*Two. Four. Eight. One. Seven.* You have five seconds to comply or you will be punished for insubordination!"

The woman Ryder had treated for a suppurating wound cleared her throat. "That's probably you, Sawbones. It's a newer number."

Ryder frowned and glanced down at the barcode on her forearm. The scabbiness of the fresh tattoo made it a bit difficult to read, but her cellmate was right. She sighed.

"Oh," she said, and clambered to her feet, joints aching after the night spent on the cold concrete floor. "Brilliant."

The female guards glared daggers at her as she cracked her spine with a series of pops and moved toward the door.

"Turn around. Present your wrists through the gap."

They cuffed her.

"So," she asked casually. "What's on the agenda for this morning? Mandatory counseling session? Vocational rehabilitation?" She paused looking between the two. "Table tennis?"

"Morning exercise session," said the shorter one, her expression unchanging.

Jeers and shouts erupted from inside the cell.

"I can hardly wait." Ryder had only been two days into her stint as fake prison doctor when she'd heard the first whispers about guards and other low-level employees betting on staged prisoner fights. This morning, there was little doubt in her mind about who would be topping the bill.

"Someone really has it in for me, huh?" she asked.

Shorty turned, eyeing her up and down. "Yes," she said.

Ryder shut her mouth and gritted her teeth as the guards marched her along toward who-knew-what kind of fresh clusterfuck.

⸻ ✦ ⸻

Upon arrival at the exercise yard, the guards had removed Temple's muzzle and restraints before shoving him through the entrance gate and slamming it shut behind him. He staked out a small corner of the open area, which was about the size of a basketball or hoverball court, bounded by a ten-foot chain-link fence topped with coils of razor wire that were probably electrified.

A conspicuously placed weapon array loomed down from the top of a tall pole situated in such a way as to offer a clear line of fire across the entire area. There were also jet nozzles placed at intervals along the top of the fence that could, Temple knew, spew plumes of anaesthetizing gas over the yard.

The dozen or so human men trapped inside the confined area with him were twitchy. Restless. Temple leaned against the fence with his arms crossed in front of his chest—a casual stance, but one which emphasized both his height and the muscle mass he had managed to maintain, even after weeks spent in a tiny cell with insufficient food and water.

His physique wasn't as impressive as it had been when he was captured, but he'd made a point of keeping up with basic stretching and a small amount of cardio—as much as possible within the confined space of his cell. Both were things that minimized unnecessary caloric expenditure while maximizing his ability to use his remaining strength if and when it became necessary. So far, no one in this group had shown any inclination to fuck with him.

In a place like this, the animal brain was a strong influence. They were all human. They were all male. There were no resources here, and hence, no reason to fight. Movement as someone came toward him caught his eye, followed a moment later by a shock of surprise.

"Temple?" asked a ginger-haired kid with a vaguely familiar face. "Temple, man, is that really you? What the fuck you doing here, bro?"

Temple straightened from his slouch and snapped his fingers, pointing at the boy as a name popped up to go with the face. "Jonah, right? From the Backway?"

Jonah's face lit up. "Yeah, man! It is you!"

Glossing over Jonah's earlier question about why he was here, Temple dropped an arm across Jonah's shoulder and gave it a friendly squeeze. "What the hell are you in here for, kid? Didn't I tell you to keep your nose clean after that shit with the Southside gang?"

Jonah's face fell, and his eyes slid away. "Yeah, well. You did, but…" He took a step away, and Temple let his arm fall. "There were these guys… they were hopped up on some kind of crazy shit, and they came after Snapper. One of them had a knife and…"

He trailed off.

"Someone got killed," Temple finished for him. "And you got caught up in the sweep."

Jonah shrugged, still not looking at him.

Just then, movement outside the locked gate caught their attention, breaking the moment. One of the other men in the yard whistled, soft and low. The rest of the little crowd drew together, wolves in a pack sensing the approach of prey.

"What's going on?" Jonah asked nervously.

Temple craned his head until he could catch a glimpse of the approaching female prisoner through the chain-link, and he caught his breath. Outside stood the prison doctor with her distinctive red spikes of hair, an ugly inmate's smock replacing her lab coat and blue scrubs, and her hands cuffed behind her back.

"Son of a..." Temple cursed. He blinked and pinned Jonah with an intense gaze. "Right. Jonah— you stay back. Do not get involved in this under any circumstances, do you hear me?"

Jonah glanced back and forth between the red-haired doctor and the group of hard-eyed human men clustered in front of the gate. "Wait. They're gonna put a Vithii bitch in here with a bunch of humans? After what they tried to do to us with the bioweapon a few weeks ago? What the *fuck*?"

Temple jabbed a finger in Jonah's chest, and the teenager flinched.

"Stay. Back," Temple repeated. "I'm not fucking around, Jonah. I don't care what you see, you don't even *think* about—"

He was interrupted by the gate clanging shut behind the Vithii doctor. Her hands were free now, and she rubbed her wrists as if trying to get the circulation to return. She watched the half-circle of ragged human men arrayed around her with her chin held high, a sour expression twisting her attractive features.

"This is whacked," Jonah whispered, weaving his fingers into a section of the chain-link behind him and clasping tight.

The doctor continued to run her gaze over the men around her, as though she were assessing their strengths and weaknesses. Temple couldn't help but be impressed by the pair of giant, titanium-plated balls that the woman was apparently hauling around beneath her shapeless gray prisoner's smock.

"Well now," she said in a faux-pleasant voice. "Isn't this lovely? Don't worry, boys, I won't hurt you any more than necessary." Her lips pulled back. It wasn't a smile. "You can trust me, you know. I used to be a doctor."

FIVE

Morning dawned at Location Four, and six people once again crammed into a room that was really too small for them after Ash called them back early with news. This time, he was the one pacing, though there wasn't enough space available for the activity to be remotely satisfying.

"She's in custody, and we have a serious problem," he said tightly.

Skye made a small noise of dismay, and Kade made a louder one of disgust.

"What do you mean, 'a serious problem'?" Draven asked, not sounding any happier than Kade did.

Ash called up the hacked email with an abrupt flick of his fingers and waved a hand at it vaguely, not remotely in the mood to have to say the words out loud. The others crowded around the screen, scanning the message quickly. Ash had it memorized; especially the parts about 'mitigating this unfortunate scandal before it can reach the courts,' and 'any assistance you can render in making certain this situation goes away quietly.'

"Bastard son of a whore," Draven cursed.

Hunter lifted a hand and rubbed at his forehead before dropping it back to his side. "They're going to make her disappear. All right—we need options, and we need them now."

"We didn't even have a decent plan to get Skye's brother out," Ash said through gritted teeth. "That's why Ryder went inside in the first place."

Kade found a spot to perch nearby, resting his hip against the corner of a table piled high with hardware. He crossed his arms and frowned. "Did she relay any useful information before she was captured? Anything that would help us?"

Ash tried to organize his thoughts enough to sort through the contents of Ryder's nightly reports. "She confirmed Temple was alive and at the prison. She gave me an idea of the scope of her access to prison records, which isn't helpful now since she no longer has access. She described the general layout of the place—"

"That could be valuable," Pax offered.

Ash nodded. "I transcribed everything, and scanned the maps she sketched of the administrative wing. I'll send the attachments to your comm." He dug his fingers into his eye sockets, thinking hard. "She passed on a handful of full names of people in the chain of command there..."

"That's already public record, most likely," Hunter pointed out, and Ash nodded agreement.

"She gave me her shift schedule, which is no longer relevant," he continued, frustrated with the lack of anything really useful.

"It might still be relevant," said Pax. "If the shifts are the same across all departments, it's always useful to know when people are switching in and out. That's when a site is most vulnerable."

"All right. Let's think wider," Hunter said. "Pax. If you needed to render security at a prison ineffective during a military attack and you didn't have the forces to take it outright, what would you do?"

Pax was silent and still for a moment in that eerily machine-like way he exhibited sometimes. "Pinpoint aerial attack on the administrative offices with the goal of capturing high-level officials."

"Not practical," Kade said immediately. "We don't have the personnel. They would overrun us in no time."

Pax nodded. "Infiltration via tunnels or other means of clandestine access."

"Not enough time to find a way in, or make one," Hunter objected.

"Engineer a disturbance from the inside to act as a distraction," the cyborg suggested.

Ash perked up. "How? What kind of disturbance?"

Skye sucked in a sharp breath and straightened her spine abruptly. "A prisoner riot. What if there was a prisoner riot? Could we get in and retrieve them somehow if all the guards and security forces were busy trying to regain control of the other inmates?"

Pax looked thoughtful. "Possibly..."

Kade frowned. "How would we make that happen? And how would we prevent the guards from simply mowing down the prisoners with the automated weapons systems?"

Ash tapped his chin thoughtfully. It was easy to forget that Kade also had extensive experience with the prison in question, having been held there for longer than any of them cared to contemplate. It hadn't been the kind of information they'd originally needed—records access, administrative insight, daily operations breakdowns. But it might end up being exceptionally valuable to them under the current circumstances.

He pointed at the gray-eyed, hard-as-nails Vithii. "I need to pick your brain."

Kade raised an un-amused eyebrow. "Your funeral, *leetha*. It's not something I generally recommend."

The prison officials had kept Kade drugged into compliance with neurotonin for much of his stay, but that was only because they'd quickly learned how dangerous that sharp mind could be, even when locked inside a cell.

"Talk to me about the nuts and bolts of prisoner containment," Ash ordered, ignoring Kade's bad-tempered sniping. "Cell doors, pacification systems, security between different sections. Anything you can remember."

"It was years ago, Ash," Kade said in a flat tone. "It may be completely different now."

Frustrated, Ash flopped down in his desk chair and made a *yes, yes* motion with one hand. "Or it might not be, because bureaucracy moves at the speed of an elderly slug. What else do we honestly have to work with right now? *Ryder's chrono is ticking.*"

"He's right, *tei'laal*," Hunter said. "Just tell him what he wants to know."

Kade took a breath and blew it out slowly, visibly casting his mind back. "The individual cells are plasticrete on three sides with steel bars on the front. The door-locks are electronic, controlled by a coded keypad situated well out of arm's reach from inside the cells."

"Different codes on each?" Ash asked, reaching for a pencil stub and a scrap of paper so he could jot all this down.

"Yes, of course," Kade answered. "Each section of the prison was accessed via another coded door, along with an automatic 360-degree scanner that detected prisoner barcodes." His right hand rubbed absently at the inside of his left forearm, where Ash knew a faded prison tattoo lay half-hidden, incorporated into a sleeve of more recent tattoos. "The system was tied into a network of broad-beam weapons capable of stunning or killing, along with nozzles that sprayed anaesthetizing gas…"

Ash nodded and continued to take notes as Kade outlined what he knew of the cellblocks and adjacent prisoner areas inside the compound. When he was finished, Ash tossed the pencil aside.

"This is all computer-controlled," he said. "It's all *integrated*."

Kade looked at him, unimpressed. "You've already said you can't hack it."

"Maybe I don't need to hack it. Maybe I can get someone to plug a nice little care package directly into the system, and make every door inside that shithole pop open at once while the pacification systems quietly power down in the background." Already, his mind was churning with logic trees and computer code.

"Well," Draven said, drawing Ash's attention back to his surroundings, "I did say I'd go in if you needed me to."

Skye's reply was immediate. "I thought we agreed sending someone else in was too dangerous!"

Hating himself for what he was about to say, Ash cleared his throat. "If it was just another round of reconnaissance in hopes of getting fresh intel, I would fully agree. But if we decide to do this, then this *is* the rescue mission. It's our best shot at an end game."

Draven shrugged with that devil-may-care insouciance that made Ash want to throttle him sometimes. "I'm up for it. Just tell me what hole to stick the portable hard drive in."

Of course, it wasn't going to be *quite* that simple, but Ash was well aware that while Draven liked to play the part of the big, dumb lout, it was very much an act. And while it did pain him to let such an obvious opening for a sex joke pass unremarked, now was hardly the time. He craned around to look at their de facto leader.

"Hunter? Your call, boss," he said.

Hunter looked grim. "Kade, what percentage of the prison inmates would you say are political prisoners and non-violent offenders?"

Kade's expression grew thoughtful. "It's impossible to say. A fairly large percentage, if I had to guess. But, yes, if we pursue this plan we will undoubtedly be releasing real criminals back into the Capital."

Skye's blue eyes grew hard. "And are these criminals better or worse than the ones who hide behind grand titles and try to commit genocide against my species using bioweapons?" she asked aggressively.

As always when Hunter's little blonde sparrow of a bondmate went all hard and militant on them, Ash felt a moment of surprise—but he couldn't really disagree with the sentiment.

"I'm with Skye," he said. "We all know perfectly well that the security forces turn a blind eye to murder and assault on a regular basis when it happens inside Vithii gang territory. I refuse to feel guilty for freeing people imprisoned under a blatantly corrupt system."

Hunter glanced at the others, gauging their reactions. Kade and Pax did not offer any objections, while Draven only shrugged and said, "I've been a criminal since I was nine. Don't look at me."

"Very well," Hunter agreed. "Pax—strategic assessment?"

"Risky," Pax said. "If we do nothing, we lose both Ryder and the original target. If we pursue this course, we additionally endanger Draven, but all three gain a modest chance of escaping unharmed."

Escaping unharmed during a prison riot. Ash knew nothing of Temple beyond the fact that he'd successfully run a decoy mission inside the Regime's central government compound and lived to tell the tale, but he did know Ryder and Draven. Both of them were tough, smart, and survivors to the core. If the choice were no chance versus a fighting chance…

"Start planning for the mission," Hunter said, ending the debate. "Ash, do whatever you need to on the technological side, while the rest of us try to arrange a way in for Draven. Until he goes in, I'm open to alternate ideas, but for now, this is what we have, and this is what we'll run with."

Ash nodded, already feeling a bit overwhelmed at what needed to be done, given the timeline. "I need Kade," he said quickly.

Kade, who had been about to rise from his perch and go with the others, grunted and sank back down on the edge of the table.

"Why, *leetha*," he said, his tone dripping with heavy irony, "I didn't know you cared."

<hr>

"Hey, boys—look at that," said one of the humans surrounding Ryder, "the Vithii cow thinks she's funny! Do we think she's funny?"

Ryder sized the man up, knowing she could probably disable him, and also knowing it was unlikely these men would give her the courtesy of coming at her one at a time. Several of the others jeered, crowding forward. One olive-skinned man near the edge of the pack glared at her, his face full of anger.

"My old granny died from that shit her *Premiere* sprayed all over the city," he grated, drawling the word 'Premiere' as though it made him feel sick to say it. "I don't see much funny about her kind."

Ryder lifted her chin. "The fact that I'm on this side of the bars—and about to get the shit kicked out of me—might clue you into the fact that I'm not exactly the fuckhead-in-chief's favorite person right now. *If* you'd bother to think about it for a moment."

The man scoffed. "Aww, is that so? Right, 'cause I bet you were out there in the street protesting with the rest of us humans while that group at the water treatment plant was trying to save us. Yeah, sure you were…"

It was all Ryder could do not to let a bark of bitter laughter escape.

Oh, she thought, *you really have no idea.*

Unfortunately, the last thing she could afford was for someone here to realize she had ties with Hunter or any of the others. As far as she knew, no one had made the connection between her identity as Aryderlyn Erisuel and her connection to the Shadow Wing. That was very much how she intended to keep it. She would not give up information on her comrades, but she wasn't stupid enough to think she could stand up to Regime interrogation techniques, either. Not once they brought out the drugs, and the machines.

"I'm a doctor," she told the human, "and I did everything in my power to save lives."

The first half of that statement was a lie. The second half was true. Judging by the expressions around her, neither half was believed.

"Ooh, a *doctor*," crooned the first man who had spoken. "Why don't you come over here, *doc*? I've got an ache, and I bet you can make it *all better*."

He walked forward as he spoke, and reached a hand toward her. She batted it away, probably with more force than was necessary. He smiled, a slow, dangerous grin.

"Feisty, eh? Good thing I've got a bunch of buddies here to help hold you down."

Ryder tried to watch the rest of the group with her peripheral vision while keeping her main focus on the two most immediate threats. Several of the others looked uncomfortable. A few looked curious, and a couple looked downright enthusiastic. Bottom line—she was hemmed in near the locked gate, and would probably only be able to take out two or three of these men before getting her ass handed to her.

Humans weren't known for being all that impressive in the dick department. Still, the violence that went hand-in-hand with rape, combined with the power of the mob mentality, meant that they were likely to do some significant damage before the guards decided to haul her carcass out of the exercise yard.

She'd have to take a stab at fighting, and then play unconscious when and if they got the upper hand on her. Lack of any sort of feedback from the victim might dissuade some of the ones who were on the fence regarding sexual assault, and hopefully dial down the overall violence level.

She could deal with the psychological fallout later, if she survived.

It was ironic that the one time her *grei'kaapt* pheromones might come in truly handy for something, she was surrounded by a species with the wrong kind of endoreceptors.

Movement on the left side of the group caught her eye, and a dark-skinned man—unusually tall for a human—shoved one of the others out of the way and strode to her side. He faced off with Lead Rapist, as she'd come to mentally label the wiry brown-haired man who'd tried to lay a hand on her. With a shock, she recognized her would-be patient from yesterday.

Temple Akenzua. Skye's foster brother.

She scowled at him, trying to figure out what in the prophets' names he thought he was doing.

"Lay off," he said, his eyes flicking from the man in front of him to the one whose grandparent had been killed. "We're not animals. You know the guards place bets on this shit, right?"

"Fuck you, race traitor," snarled Lead Rapist, dazzling Ryder with the brilliance of his clever riposte.

Then, he swung for Temple's head, while two other humans charged at her. Ryder dodged the first and used his momentum to plow him face-first into the metal fence. Temple blocked his opponent's first blow and turned his shoulder into the second. She tangled an arm with her other attacker and jammed a hard knee between his legs while snapping, "What do you think you're doing, you idiot? I just fixed that chest wound!"

Her unexpected ally shot her an odd look. "The hell you did. You should've finished the damn job—" He jabbed a fist into Lead Rapist's gut, doubling the man over. "—instead of walking off in the middle of it!"

With that, he hit his opponent with a vicious head-butt, sending him sprawling.

Several of the men were still wavering, unsure whether to wade into the brawl or not. A couple more did, and Ryder heard Temple grunt as a blow to his torso jarred the half-healed slash across his pectoral. He shook it off, and Ryder had to admit that Skye's foster brother was a decent fighter to have around in a scrape.

Even without his rich, brown skin and black dreadlocks, no one would ever have mistaken him for Skye's biological sibling. He moved like a graceful predator, and while Skye was good with a blaster, her general level of physical adroitness was less 'jungle cat' and more 'newborn calf.'

Ryder winced as a fist caught her in the side, and crashed an elbow down on the man's shoulder in retaliation. More of the humans looked on the verge of jumping into the fray, and the situation was in danger of sliding into complete chaos when a skinny human kid with freckled skin and orange hair jumped between the men who were fighting and the ones still weighing their choices.

"Stop!" yelled the youngster, throwing his hands up in a halting gesture. "What are we *doing*? Fighting each other?"

"Get out of the way, Jonah," said one of the non-combatants—not unkindly.

At the same instant, Temple snapped, "Jonah, I told you to *stay back*!"

The rain of blows paused, Temple and Ryder's current opponents both frozen with their fists drawn back as the simultaneous protective gesture from both sides of the brawl penetrated the tense atmosphere. Ryder held her breath, poised to block or duck.

"*What are we doing*?" Jonah asked again, a plaintive note in his voice. "This is *bullshit*."

Evidently, none of the humans here had been heavily involved in debate team during their educations, but something about Jonah's scathing tone combined with his obvious youth and relative vulnerability seemed to be doing the job. Temple's opponent shoved away from him, backing a few steps away.

The man who had Ryder by the front of her smock still stood poised.

"Get off her, man," Jonah said. "*Seriously*."

"Yeah, come on, just step away," agreed the human who had told Jonah to get out of the way a moment ago. "Look, she's not worth it. I don't wanna be cheap entertainment for the damned guards."

Ryder debated saying something conciliatory or persuasive, but decided instead to just keep her mouth shut. The rough hand tangled in the gray polysynth of her smock loosened, one finger at a time. She stepped out of reach, her back brushing the chain-link of the fence.

"Thank you," she said gruffly, even though the words rankled. She flicked her eyes from Temple to Jonah and back. To her surprise, Temple moved closer until he was once again standing shoulder to shoulder with her.

"For what? I didn't do anything," he muttered, and Ryder had to stifle an incredulous snort.

His wound was bleeding sluggishly again, and the corner of her mouth twisted. Something about having been interrupted before she could properly finish that job annoyed her immensely. She heard noises and glanced around. Outside the fence, several people were approaching.

Thinking fast, she said, "Don't react," in a voice hopefully too low to be picked up by guards or surveillance equipment. Temple's eyebrows drew together in confusion, and she continued, "You and I share a family member, Temple Akenzua. I guess it must be a small world beneath that wide Ilarian… *sky*."

Temple's dark, heavy-lidded eyes went wide, and his lips parted. She gave him a sharp shake of her head, afraid he would ignore her warning and say something incriminating. He continued to stare at her, something about that intense gaze holding her captive longer than was wise under the present circumstances.

Finally, she managed to tear her gaze away—but only when the approaching footsteps came to a halt on the other side of the metal gate, and a male throat was cleared. Ice water ran down Ryder's spine as a voice she'd never wanted to hear again said, "Well now, Lyn… my little pet. Still causing trouble after all this time?"

SIX

Ryder's heart sped up, though she tried not to react outwardly as she turned to see Jodor Erisuel, the Regime's Under-Minister of Military Logistics, standing outside the fence.

Her bondmate.

"My name is not Lyn," she said, even as her mating bond tried to pull her toward him like some kind of needy, pathetic limpet. "And I am not your pet."

He looked exactly the same as she remembered—strong jaw, heavy brow, light brown hair buzzed close at the sides of his head and rising into longer spikes on top. His eyes were still distant and cruel; his back was still ramrod straight. She still hated him for what he'd done to her, and she hated her body for not giving a damn that he'd discarded her like trash and tried to have her killed because her desperate, grief-fueled actions were an inconvenience to his career.

Beside her, Temple tensed. She silently willed him not to draw attention to himself.

Ryder had been so focused on the face from her past that she hadn't taken note of the other figures flanking Jodor. She recognized the Intendant next, but there was an unfamiliar Vithii woman standing next to him as well. She was striking— slender by Vithii standards, with hair so pale it looked almost white. She was young, though—not old. Perhaps a few years younger than Ryder, and not nearly so weathered by hard living. She wore a tailored trouser suit in charcoal gray, an official-looking badge pinned to one perfectly turned lapel.

"Why is this woman grouped in with male humans?" the woman asked sharply. "This is against prison protocol. Remove her from the enclosure immediately."

Ryder lifted an eyebrow, taken aback. The rule-stickler's accent wasn't Ilarian. It was Vitharan. She was from the Vithii homeworld. The Intendant stiffened, but after a moment he jerked his chin toward two of the female guards, who moved to unlock the gate and retrieve Ryder from the tense standoff in the exercise yard. Temple made an abortive move as if he might reach for her, but stopped himself, frustration clear in his expression.

"Of course, Ambassador Veila'ana," said the Intendant in a stiff tone, "I'm certain it was merely an oversight. No doubt one of the guards became confused about the prisoners' exercise rota."

Ambassador Veila'ana turned striking green eyes on the man. "This is how accidents happen, Intendant." She brushed past him and clasped her fingers around Ryder's bare forearm. Ryder felt an odd shock, as though static electricity had discharged between them, and she tensed.

Those piercing green eyes pinned hers for a moment, and Ryder thought she detected... surprise? It was covered in an instant, however, and the woman said, "There, now. Are you injured? Tell me, what crime are you incarcerated for?"

"I'm fine," Ryder said, ignoring what was probably at least a couple of bruised ribs, "and I have no idea why they're holding me. I haven't been formally charged with anything."

"Not true," Jodor said calmly. "This woman was charged with several very serious crimes in absentia eight years ago—most notably unlicensed medical experimentation on a child, resulting in death."

The aching stab of guilt was so strong Ryder's knees nearly gave out. The ambassador jerked her hand away from Ryder's arm as though she'd been burned, reminding her again that she was untouchable; the lowest of the low. She could feel the disgust rolling off the humans still locked inside the enclosure without even turning to look. No doubt they were wishing they'd piled onto the fight and ripped her head off when they had the chance.

"I see," said the Vitharan woman, after an awkward beat. "Well… now that this unfortunate error with the exercise rota has been caught and rectified, I imagine you'll be taking her back to her cell? When is her hearing scheduled?"

Jodor's mouth flattened into a thin line. It was an expression Ryder still found shockingly familiar after all this time. She wanted to make some cutting remark—*Yes, Under-Minister Erisuel… when is my hearing scheduled? Oh, what's that? You didn't bother scheduling it since you assumed the Intendant would be able to arrange a convenient accident for me before then?*

But it was no good. It was all she could do to stand there trying not to tremble while the past rose up to swallow the present, as though the intervening eight years had never happened.

Her bondmate's expression never wavered. "The dockets are very busy right now. We're still waiting on a date."

A noise of disbelief escaped Ryder's throat, sounding choked.

Veila'ana's eyes flickered between them, almost too quick to catch. With a nod of sympathy, she brushed her fingers briefly over Jodor's hand in a supportive gesture. "I can tell this must be very hard for you. I'm sure you're already looking into counsel, but if you need a good attorney I can offer some recommendations."

Fortunately for the ambassador, Jodor appeared to have very little interest in her despite her striking looks. *Count yourself lucky, girl*, Ryder thought. *In fact, you should get off this shithole of a planet while you can, and run right back to Vithara. You have no idea what you're dealing with.*

"I'll keep it in mind," Jodor told her, in enough of a dismissive tone that she seemed to get the hint and back off.

"He might not be interested, but I am," Ryder managed, finally finding her tongue again. It was a lie—Ryder couldn't involve a lawyer, since a lawyer would be legally compelled to inform the authorities if they discovered her connection with Hunter and the others. Still, it might be an excuse for future contact with this off-world ambassador, and the more people who had an interest in Ryder not ending up on a slab, the better.

Indeed, Veila'ana seemed to brighten a bit. "Certainly. I'll arrange for visitation in the next day or two and bring you the contact information."

The Intendant looked at Ryder uneasily, and she knew he was feeling the pinch of being caught between two powerful people who wanted conflicting things from him. Jodor, an influential Regime official, wanted Ryder gone. Veila'ana, an off-world diplomat, wanted every rule followed. While Ryder…

Ryder wanted desperately for none of this to be happening. Without consciously intending to do it, she looked back at Temple, the reason she was in this place. He was frowning, his fingers tangled in the chain-link fence, looking at her as though he was trying to see straight through to the inside of her skull and the secrets buried there.

She had no idea how to save him.

She couldn't even save herself.

As Temple was herded back to his cell, nursing a new round of bruises, strains, and scrapes, he tried to still his whirling thoughts enough to make sense of what had just happened. First and foremost, Skye was alive.

Skye was fucking *alive*.

Could he really afford to believe it? He'd hoped for it. Prayed for it, to gods and prophets he barely believed in. But what gossip filtered in through the prison walls was vague and riddled with contradictions. His biggest cause for optimism had been the fact that his jailers were keeping him around and relatively intact. He knew they knew who he was, so the most obvious reason to hold onto him was so they could use him as leverage, either against Skye or against their father Zarian.

He held out far less hope for his foster father. The Regime had no tolerance for insubordination within the ranks, and they would have known as soon as he and Skye ran that Zarian had betrayed them. He wasn't sure about Stella, Zarian's wife. The Premiere had been holding her as leverage against him, but Temple had asked around as much as he'd been able, and there was no sign that she was being kept here in this prison.

In truth, neither he nor Skye had ever had much use for the woman, but it still nagged at him. Not that he could do anything to help her, even if he knew where she was. And that brought him back full circle. Could Skye do anything? Had the red-haired Vithii doctor been here because Skye sent her? If so, they were as fucked as ever, because apparently she'd only made it a few days before getting captured.

But then, there was also that creepy Minister of whatever-the-shit. Not to mention the slightly less creepy but still decidedly odd ambassador chick. The gods-damned undercurrents in this place were developing undercurrents. No way could Minister Slimeball have been telling the truth about the charges against Red. No *fucking* way.

And yet... the way she had looked when he said it, like someone just stabbed her through the heart and all that was keeping her on her feet was sheer stubbornness. She'd stared down a dozen men who wanted to lynch her, and bantered with Temple about his chest wound while knocking heads together like a professional fighter. But as soon as that Vithii asshole had shown up, the blood drained from her face as if she'd seen a ghost.

Prophets. If the fucker *had* been telling the truth about what she'd done, she was the worst kind of monster… and yet he still couldn't stop thinking about her.

She was either a monster, or she was a messenger from Skye. Maybe it was a moot point. He had no way to contact her again. No way to find out more about why she was here. And despite the ambassador's bizarre intervention in the matter, the Vithii minister looked like a man who would do whatever it took to get what he wanted.

Right now, it looked to Temple like he wanted Red gone.

⸻◆⸻

Location Four had become a hub of buzzing activity over the past few hours, as people came and went, arranging logistics and trying to cobble together a crazy mission with no decent lead time.

"Ash," Pax said, "we need to discuss contingency plans."

Ash ground his teeth together, not looking up from the lines of code that were starting to blur in his vision. "Take it up with Hunter. I don't have a Plan B, Pax. I barely have a Plan A." He blinked, trying to bring the screen back into focus. "Kade. Why is there a for/next loop on line sixty-one-twenty-three of this program? And is Draven back yet?"

Kade gave him a flat stare. "A for/next loop? Why are you asking me? You put it there. And yes, he got back half a cycle ago."

Ash glared at the screen until he found the place where two lines of code had been juxtaposed, and fixed it. "Then somebody get him in here! I need to set him up with a fake identity chip while this is compiling—"

"And I need an estimate of the likelihood that your software will fail, before I can work on those contingency plans we were talking about," Pax interrupted implacably.

Without thinking, Ash slammed a palm down on the edge of the desk and glared at the cyborg who could snap him in two as easily as breaking a matchstick. "An estimate? How about we call it fifty-fifty? It will either work, *or it won't.*"

Pax continued to look at him without expression. Ash realized that his hands were trembling, something that had started afflicting him at odd moments during the past few god-awful weeks. He closed his eyes for the span of a few heartbeats, breathing slowly.

"Look, Pax—I know you're worried. We're all bloody worried. I don't know if the damned software will work, because I'm repurposing it from something completely different and I have no way to test it to determine the likely failure rate. All right?"

Pax gave a short nod and buggered off, presumably to find Hunter and decide what to do if Ash's code ended up being a useless crock of shit. He turned back to Kade. "So. Draven?"

"Already sorted."

Ash scowled at him. "What do you mean, 'already sorted'?"

Kade glowered back. "Keep up. What do you think I mean? I took care of it. You're not the only techworm I know, Ash. Keep your mind on your code or this whole thing will be a waste of time, not to mention a waste of a talented medic."

His hands started to shake harder, and Ash gripped the edge of the desk to stop them. "I want to see that identichip before he tries to use it."

"*Fine*, leetha." Kade eyed him up and down before rising from his seat. "And thank you so much for your touching confidence in the rest of us. I need a fucking injection. I'll be back."

Kade stalked out, the door closing solidly behind him. Ash slumped in his chair and jammed the heel of his hand into his right eye socket, trying to squeeze out the headache that had taken up residence. A few moments later, the door opened and closed quietly, admitting Skye. She looked like hell, pale with dark circles under her bloodshot eyes. Her tired gaze scanned him in almost exactly the same way Kade's had.

"How long since you slept?" she asked without preamble.

He thought back, failed to come up with the number of cycles since he'd caught a catnap under his desk, and said, "It hardly matters. It's not as though there's time for a beauty rest right now."

She continued to stare at him. "You need to take a break."

His mouth twisted down. "I just told you—"

"Stop," she interrupted. "You *need*. To *take*. A *break*. I didn't say you needed to go to sleep, though you clearly do. Get away from that fucking computer screen, eat something, drink something, then go to the lav and splash some water on your face. You look like shit." Her blue eyes tracked down from his face to the desktop. "And your hands are shaking."

They squared off silently for several beats before she added, "Ash, *please*," and he crumpled like a wet dishrag.

"Just… for a few minutes," he said. "And I need you to convince Draven to let me look at the ID chip Kade got for him. I'm not sending him into that prison with something I haven't checked personally."

She nodded, and then surprised the hell out of him by crossing the distance to his chair and wrapping her arms around him, squeezing tight. He froze, covering a flinch when her palm fell on one of the bruises decorating his back.

"Ooh—don't tell Hunter about our little secret, sweetheart," he joked weakly. "He'll rip my head off and use it to play hoverball."

She huffed at him. "I think he knows I'm not really your type, Ash. Besides, if he kills you, who's he going to call when he needs someone to hijack radio transmissions and write prison-riot viruses on the fly?"

Ash closed his eyes and let himself lean into her slender body for the space of a few breaths—hating the weakness, but needing the feeling of human warmth against his skin without the ever-present, looming series of crises and catastrophes that seemed to comprise his existence these days.

Skye's chest rose and fell, like she was steeling herself for something. "I know what you've been doing to get intel for us, Ash. It doesn't take a degree in rocket science to figure it out. I… wish you wouldn't."

Ash stiffened and eased away, feeling the deep ache flare in his back as he did. "I'm sure I have no idea what you mean, Skye. All you need to play the intel game is a silver tongue and a quick mind, both of which I possess in spades. Now, I promise to go eat something and rest my eyes for a few minutes. Do you promise to lure Draven and his identichip in here for me when I get back?"

Skye watched him sadly for a long moment. "Sure. I promise," she said, and left him to it with a final backward glance.

When she was gone, he slumped forward for a moment, resting his head in his shaking hand… wondering how long they'd be able to keep up this insanity before it caught up with one or more of them for good. Wondering if it would be his fault—his mistake—when it finally did.

SEVEN

No one bothered Ryder for the rest of the day, or the night that followed. She'd been taken to a private cell—little more than a plasticrete box that barely measured two meters by two meters. There, she debated the merits of eating the colorless slop that passed for prison food when the guard slid it through the gap at the bottom of the barred door. She sniffed it and pulled back in distaste. The stuff smelled decidedly off. Remembering the woman with dysentery in the communal cell, she decided against taking the chance.

The bucket of stale, lukewarm water was a risk, too, but she'd lose her strength a lot faster by becoming dehydrated than she would by skipping a few meals. Her ribcage sported a deep bruise where one of the human men's fists had connected, and the pain when she breathed in too deeply told her that she'd torn something.

Could be worse. Could be broken, she thought resignedly.

The absolute lack of any sort of mental stimulation was the worst part of this stretch of relative peace and quiet. Normally, it wouldn't have bothered her. She'd always tended toward introversion, and was perfectly capable of entertaining herself when the need arose. This situation bore no relation whatsoever to normalcy, though. Every few minutes her thoughts would drift back to Jodor, and the burning bitterness she felt over what he'd done to her.

No doubt he hated her every bit as much as she hated him. She'd ruined Jodor's carefully constructed plans for a perfect life, throwing messy emotions and complications all over it. Not to mention the pall of scandal she'd draped across his career.

How lucky were those couples who were never tested… who never had to step off the ledge and find out if someone was waiting below to catch them? And how much luckier were those who weathered the storm and emerged into the sunlight together, stronger than ever? She thought of Hunter and Skye. In some ways, she envied them. In other ways, the two of them terrified her.

Right now, a fairly large part of her wanted to find a convenient sharp object and hack the twisted, atrophied mating gland right out of her fucking neck. How dare any part of her still be drawn to a person who wanted her dead? A person who had actively tried to have her killed? Bloody *biology*. Every fucked-up thing that had happened to her in the past ten years had hinged on *biology*. She'd become a doctor to tame it, but instead it had ripped her life apart and taken away everything she used to value.

She angrily poured the contents of the bowl down the stinking hole in the floor used for waste, and shoved it back outside through the slot in the bars. She couldn't afford to let this place get to her. She couldn't afford to let *Jodor* get to her. She had to keep her wits about her.

Instead, she focused on the Vitharan ambassador. Something about her seemed… *off*… but her presence here was still very interesting. Ilarius wasn't a fortress. The planet was part of the Seven Systems, though the Premiere's strategy to seize power included instituting a degree of isolationism. Even so, they still had ambassadors from other planets. But none, to Ryder's knowledge, who hung out in the prison system lending aid to random prisoners.

For all that the mysterious Veila'ana had made the hair on Ryder's neck stand up with her casually familiar touch outside the exercise yard, she still wanted to see the woman again and try to gather more details about who she was and what she was doing here. Ryder wondered if she would follow through on the promise to meet with her on the pretense of handing over contact information for a good lawyer.

As if a good lawyer would be able to help me now, Ryder thought acerbically.

Hours passed, her thoughts circling ceaselessly back to Jodor and how very, very fucked she was, despite her every attempt to drag her attention away and focus on other things. Finally—around midday, she thought—guards arrived at her cell, the familiar clang of a shock wand hitting the metal bars jolting her out of her fugue.

"Face the back wall. Present your wrists for manacles. You have a visitor."

Ryder complied, relieved beyond measure to have something happen that would hopefully keep her from going out of her thrice-damned mind before the sun even set in the unseen sky beyond the prison walls.

Draven waited in front of the administrative entrance of the Capital prison as the workers reporting for the morning shift filed through the security queue. He might not *enjoy* dangerous missions, as such, but he did prefer them to sitting around on his ass like a useless piece of shit while one of his friends was in danger. For that reason, he was happy enough to be standing in front of the glass doors while the red lines of a full-body scan played over him. A short distance away, a bored-looking security goon checked his forged identichip.

He wasn't particularly worried about the system flagging it; not after Ash had combed over the thing with that obsessive, single-minded focus he was prone to when he hadn't been getting enough sleep. Sometimes, Draven worried that the reckless human bastard was going to go completely off the rails one of these days, with his self-destructive bullshit and his gods-damned martyr complex.

Sometimes, Draven wanted to throttle him, or shake him until his teeth rattled and he stopped signing up to do stupid and dangerous things in the name of *gathering intel*. Then, Draven started to worry that Ash might actually enjoy that kind of a brawl... or that *he* might... and the idea quickly lost any appeal it originally had.

Yesterday, Skye had slipped in to speak with Ash privately for a few minutes, and apparently succeeded in talking him off the ledge for the time being. Or at least, she'd talked him into eating something and catching a couple hours' sleep overnight while the final round of code was compiling.

Skye was all right. Hunter had done well for himself there, even if she was human. Not that there was anything wrong with that, *per se*— Draven just didn't really understand how it would work… a Vithii and a human. *Logistically*, like. They seemed to have it figured out, though, and he knew it wasn't really any of his business anyway.

The ping of the scanner completing its pass drew him out of his thoughts.

"All good?" he asked—casual, as though he didn't have a care in the world on his first day as part of the project to replace the cracked conduits housing electrical and data cables within the prison walls.

In reality, he might've had a few cares. But probably not as many cares as the guy currently unconscious and under guard in the basement of one of Kade's commercial hangars… the guy whose job Draven was stealing for a day. Whether that job would still exist tomorrow depended largely on how effective Ash's viral program ended up being. That program was etched into a data wafer buried under the skin of Draven's forearm, encased in a thin pouch of electromagnetic jamming material. The lack of any beeping alarms from the scanner meant that stage one of the plan had apparently worked, at least.

"Yeah, you're good to go," said the security goon. "You know where you're supposed to report in for your shift, right?"

"Yep," Draven said, though in reality he had no idea and didn't particularly care. Right now, cable conduits didn't interest him nearly as much as the computers they were hooked to.

"Go on, then," said the goon, waving him past the checkpoint to the glass and steel doors beyond. "Remember, all tools remain on site, and will be counted and logged at the beginning and end of every shift."

Draven lifted his hand in lazy acknowledgment and headed inside. Even on the admin side, the prison was anal as hell about people bringing in any items that might conceivably be used as a weapon if they ended up in the hands of a prisoner. Which made perfect sense, obviously. It just also happened to be a major pain in Draven's ass right now.

The door swung shut behind him, leaving him in the lobby of the employee's entrance of the administration wing. This was the same entrance Ryder had used on each of the four days before she'd been compromised. She'd jotted down rough maps of all the areas she'd had access to, and sent them to Ash each night when she reported in after her shift was over.

Unfortunately, the area Draven needed to get to wasn't the same area where Ryder had worked. The prison infirmary straddled the boundary between the prison itself and the admin wing. Judging by the publicly available records of building plans and utility layouts that Ash and Kade had managed to lay their hands on, the servers and tech hub were on the opposite end of the wing.

Again, it made sense. If they weren't careful, someone might wander into that control center and cause *all sorts* of problems. A smirk pulled up one corner of Draven's lips.

He walked with purpose in the general direction of where the computer hub must logically be.

The trick to this kind of shit was not that you needed to have any kind of clue where you were going. The trick was to make it look like you knew *exactly* where you were going. Given the life he'd led, Draven had more cause than most to appreciate the importance of appearances.

As he had expected, no one questioned his right to be there. Why would they? If he was here, he'd already been through the security point. And if he'd already been through the security point, he obviously belonged here.

Idiots.

The lifts were exactly where you'd expect lifts to be in a place like this. And, like in every office ever built anywhere, there was a helpful list posted nearby, outlining which departments were on which floors. Draven entered the first lift when it arrived, joining a Vithii woman with a neat suit and a jaded expression, along with a janitor wearing earbuds who was swaying back and forth to music only he could hear.

Draven mashed the button for the third floor and pasted a surly expression on his face to ensure that neither of them would try to engage him in conversation.

So, lovely weather we're having, isn't it? Yes, there's hardly any haze left over from the Premiere's bioweapon attack at all today.

Needless to say, small talk in the Capital had become a bit stilted over the last few weeks.

The door dinged for the third floor and Draven got off. Again, a helpful sign with arrows on it directed him toward the department he needed. As he got closer, the pleasant beige walls and carpet gave way to sterile white with tile floors. The signs degenerated from friendly directions like 'Re-strooms' and 'Cafeteria' to techno-speak like 'Type-E Microprocessor Servers' and 'Integral Fluid-Link Control Room.'

Draven headed for the servers, not pausing when the guard stationed outside the door came into view. "Hey," he said, once he was within speaking distance. "Sorry, I think I'm turned around. It's my first day and I'm supposed to be with the crew working on the conduits. The guy at the door told me they were on the third floor but I'm starting to think he actually meant the second floor—"

The flood of words had brought him to within arm's length of the guard, who opened his mouth to answer. He was met by Draven's fist, and fell like a stone before he got the first word out. Draven caught him and lowered him silently, grabbing his sidearm. A quick search of his pockets didn't come up with anything else that looked terribly useful, but Draven did pocket his ID badge and comm unit, just in case.

Checking the settings on the compact blaster, he ensured it was set to stun and shot the guard to make certain he stayed down for a bit. Then, he entered the room beyond and stunned everyone in it as they cried out and tried to scramble up from their desk chairs. There were four techs in the main room and a fifth hiding in the little break room off to the side.

He arranged them lying on their sides in case they threw up when the stun beam started to wear off. They might've sold out to a corrupt government, but for all he knew, they were nice people other-wise. They probably had families and kids back home. He'd feel bad if any of them accidentally choked to death simply because he needed unfettered access to their computer system for a few minutes.

Draven knew there were security cameras running all over the prison complex, so he didn't have much time. He glanced around, looking for anything sharp enough to cut skin, and silently cursed the place's paranoia about sharp objects falling into prisoners' hands. His eyes lit on a tape dispenser sitting on a desk. The serrated metal cutting edge wasn't properly sharp, but it would be slightly better than trying to use a fucking ballpoint pen to dig the data wafer out of his arm, and ending up with the world's stupidest self-administered tattoo afterward.

He popped the metal strip free of the plastic dispenser and sat down on the closest chair. The wafer in its little EM-protective pouch itched and burned under his skin. He had to saw at his forearm for several seconds before the dull metal teeth of the blade finally caught and drew blood. By the time he managed to squeeze the little packet out of the shallow, jagged wound he was cursing whoever's idea it had originally been. Probably Ash's... or maybe Kade's.

He bet Ryder would've been able to come up with something better. Yet another reason they needed her back. Draven muttered under his breath and wiped the blood off of his hand and the pouch holding the wafer, then tore the EM-masking material open with his teeth.

The wafer seemed unharmed, at least. Draven glanced around and went to the first terminal he saw that was still showing active and logged in. He maneuvered the desk chair around the body of the employee lying slumped on her side at its base. The terminal was one of the newer flat-screen models with all of the ports located on the back. He confirmed that there was a wafer port and set the terminal back into place, clicking through screens until he got to the user interface for the file architecture.

Thank all the gods and prophets, someone had exercised the good sense to label everything in understandable Standard—there was nothing more fun than wading through a file system where everything was named with cryptic combinations of letters and numbers. He was able to dig down into the system until he found the program that ran the security protocols on the prison side, and once he had it pulled up, he slid the wafer into place in its slot.

He let it download and dumped the files into the security folder, then double-clicked the executable file Ash had labeled 'load-this-shit.exe.' A blue loading icon circled just about long enough for Draven to start to get nervous. The window went black, then white. After another interminable pause, an orange button appeared, with the words 'LOAD UPDATE?' in blocky letters.

"Yes, fucking please," Draven grumbled, and clicked the button.

That was the extent of his part; the rest was up to the virus and Ash's programming skills. He flipped off the display so the screen showed black even though the terminal itself was still running. He also unplugged the keyboard, leaving the cable where it was so anyone trying to mess with it would have to figure out what was wrong and plug it back in before they could do anything else.

Draven didn't wait around to see what happened next. He left the room, checking the corridor in both directions before stepping over the stunned guard and jogging off in the opposite direction than where he'd come from. A shout came from the junction behind him and he whirled, shooting down the two guards who appeared. This time, he didn't hang around long enough to arrange their bodies in the recovery position.

Shit was about to hit the turbo prop, and he didn't particularly want to end up being around when it did. Someone would find the guards soon enough.

The security forces would almost certainly be expecting Draven to head for an exit. And that, of course, was why he was heading straight into the heart of the prison. Well, that, and the fact that both Ryder and Skye's brother were also in the heart of the prison. This part of what he was doing… might not have been exactly in line with the plan as previously discussed.

Draven respected the shit out of Hunter, but Hunter should also have known Draven well enough by now to realize that there was no way he was going to go hide in the fucking basement while Ryder was fighting for her life in the middle of a prison riot. He might be able to find her and he might not. But he was armed, and she wasn't, so he had to try.

Besides, if he managed to find her and something happened to him, this way he'd have a doctor handy. Really, as plans went, it was entirely logical.

The others were stationed at various points around the prison where they could keep an eye on all of the building's exits. It wasn't a perfect setup—

there was likely to be chaos once the riot started—but it was the best they could come up with. Pax was still spitting metaphorical nails at the absence of any real contingency plan. Not that Draven could really blame him; he was all for backup plans, especially when his ass was one of the ones on the line.

Even so, Draven couldn't really remember ever seeing the cyborg so on edge before. The others bought into the whole 'cyborgs don't have emotions' thing, but sometimes Draven wasn't so sure. Cyborgs also weren't supposed to question orders or have the capacity to disobey their superiors, but apparently Pax had missed that memo. Draven sincerely hoped he'd have the chance to see Pax's reaction to having Ryder returned to them safe and whole.

Another guard appeared ahead of him and Draven shot her down. He suspected that most of the guards in the admin wing would be called in to deal with the prisoners before long, assuming the program was running as it was supposed to. It would be worth keeping that thought in mind, certainly. Depending on conditions, it might be safer to come back here and get out of the prison the way he'd come in. He doubted most of the other prisoners would think to try the admin entrances, since they didn't have any real knowledge of this side of the complex.

Draven arrived at a T-junction and flattened his back against the wall, peering cautiously around the corner in both directions. To his right, several guards were jogging away from him, heading for the inmate areas as predicted. A short, dangerous smile graced his features for only a moment. The program was working.

He waited until the guards disappeared from view, and followed them toward the chaos.

EIGHT

Ryder sat at the heavy table in one of the rooms used for visitations. Her hands were chained to durasteel rings welded to the table frame, and the cold metal seat of the chair was chilling her ass through the light polysynth smock.

Veila'ana sat across the table from her, legs crossed and hands folded neatly before her. "You interest me," she said in that heavy homeworld accent.

"Do I?" Ryder asked in a sour tone. "I assure you, I'm not really that interesting."

The ambassador laughed, a clear sound that seemed desperately out of place in these surroundings. Ryder realized she couldn't remember the last time she'd laughed like that. She suspected it had been more than eight years ago, certainly.

Sobering, Veila'ana regarded her for a long moment. "You appear remarkably blasé for a *grei'kaapt* female whose former mate wants her to disappear."

So the other woman *had* picked up on the subtext yesterday when she'd stepped in to get Ryder out of the exercise yard and back to relative safety. Ryder cautiously tried to feel her out a bit further.

"*Blasé*? Again, I assure you… I'm really not."

Veila'ana met her eyes and held them. "I know."

Ryder nodded. "Then you know a good lawyer won't help me—even if Jodor doesn't manage to run them off before the trial even starts."

"You don't really expect to get to trial at all, do you?" Veila'ana asked.

Ryder didn't even pause. "No."

The ambassador tilted her head like a bird. "Are you guilty of the charges against you?"

"Yes."

Veila'ana opened her mouth to speak, but before she could, a heavy clicking sound echoed through the room. Both doors creaked open, as though the locking bolts had suddenly retracted.

Ryder tensed, looking from one door to the other. "What—?"

Veila'ana lifted an eyebrow.

Two guards rushed in, weapons drawn. "Stay where you are, prisoner!" barked one.

Ryder lifted her hands, the chains clanking between them. "Yeah… I'm actually still shackled to a table, here. Not really going anywhere, am I?"

Veila'ana stood. "It was nothing the prisoner did. I've been here with her the whole time. The doors simply unlocked themselves. Perhaps a computer glitch of some sort?"

Something clicked into place in Ryder's mind, and she had to stop herself sucking in an audible breath. *Right. A computer glitch, my ass. Hunter, please tell me you're not risking anyone on a plan that crazy…*

Shouts could be heard some distance away, followed by clanging metal and the unmistakable sound of blaster fire. The guards' heads whipped around, as though they weren't sure what they should be doing. One of them wore a short-range comm unit on her hip, which crackled with static.

"Look," Veila'ana said evenly. "Maybe you should go see what's happening out there? Like the prisoner says, she's still chained to a table and she's not going anywhere. I'm armed. I can keep an eye on her if you'd like."

The guard with the comm unit appeared honestly relieved to get orders from someone who sounded like they knew what they were talking about. She nodded, her head bobbing almost comically. "Yes, ma'am. Stay here, please, until the situation is under control again and one of us comes back to relieve you."

The ambassador made a vague motion of agreement. "Certainly. I'm sure it's nothing serious."

Ryder couldn't help throwing her an *'Are you joking?'* look as the sounds of fighting grew louder in the direction of the cellblocks. The guards hurried out, leaving them alone. Veila'ana peered out through each of the doors after they'd gone, assessing the immediate surroundings before swinging them closed. The bolts still didn't catch, but it at least gave the illusion of privacy. Then, the Vitharan pulled out a compact laser pistol and aimed it at the camera in the corner. The lens exploded an instant later.

Ryder narrowed her eyes at the woman, suddenly worried that she was somehow working for Jodor after all.

"You're a member of the group that foiled the Premiere's plan to use a bioweapon on the humans," said Veila'ana.

Taken completely by surprise, Ryder flailed for a moment. *How the hell? And should she try to deny it?*

"What makes you say that?" she asked after a beat of tense silence.

"I'm not fishing, Ryder," she said, and it was the first time Ryder had heard her real name since she'd signed off the comm with Ash more than two days ago. "I'm stating fact. Quickly, now. There's no time."

"Did the others send you?" Ryder couldn't help asking.

"Your comrades? No." She gestured at the doors. "Are they responsible for this?"

"I've no idea," Ryder told her. "It's possible."

The ambassador frowned. "If this is someone's idea of a plan, it's a reckless one."

Ryder shot her another dark look. "Really? You *think*?"

Veila'ana seemed to waver over a decision for a moment before shaking her head sharply. "All right. Hold still and keep your hands spread as wide as the cuffs will allow."

Ryder complied, barely breathing as the other woman dialed her sidearm down to the narrowest beam setting. The laser heated a small section of the chain until it glowed first red, then orange, and then white. "Pull," Veila'ana ordered, and Ryder jerked her wrists back, away from the table. The heated metal links twisted like taffy and pulled apart.

She narrowly missed branding herself on the leg when one of the broken halves of the chain slid off the table.

"We need to get out of here," the ambassador said. "If we run into guards, you're my prisoner. If we run into inmates, I'm your prisoner. We'll head for the nearest exit."

Ryder chewed her lower lip, debating for a moment before she shook her head slowly. "You should either get out or hunker down, certainly. I can't, though. I need to try to find someone first."

"Another prisoner?" Veila'ana asked, frowning. "The one you came here for?"

Unease coiled in Ryder's stomach. "You seem to know an awful lot about me for someone who claims not to have been sent by my friends."

"Yes," the Vitharan said without hesitation. "I do tend to get that reaction a lot from people." She placed a hand over Ryder's, watching her intently. "How important is this prisoner?"

Ryder had grown so unused to casual touches from her own kind over the years that she nearly jerked away out of habit before stopping herself. "Very," she said simply.

Veila'ana watched her for a moment more before she nodded and straightened. "I see. Very well. We'll both go, since I'm armed and you're not." She twisted the dial on the pistol again and threw Ryder a tight smile. "Heavy stun setting. Hopefully we won't need more than that. Now, how do you plan to find this very important prisoner?"

That was a good question. She thought about the little she knew of Temple Akenzua. He was brave. He was protective of others—he'd told the red-haired teenager to stay out of the fight in the exercise yard, and then he'd waded in to help her. He knew now that Ryder was acquainted with his foster sister.

"I'll check the areas between the cellblock housing female Vithii and the one housing humans," she decided. "He's politically important. He's almost certainly being kept in an individual cell. And he'll be looking for me, just like I'm looking for him. He has no way of knowing I'm in here in the visitor area; he'll assume I'm in with the other Vithii."

"Logical," Veila'ana said. "Also dangerous. I wonder if all the doors were affected, or only some?"

"No idea," Ryder told her. "Right now, I'm more interested in whether the automated weapons and gas systems are still online. If they are, this will be over before it's really begun." She flashed her forearm with its fresh tattoo, the skin around it still angry and red.

Veila'ana reached for the thin scarf tied loosely over the collar of her shirt. "Good point." She freed it and thrust it toward Ryder. "Tie this around your forearm to confuse the scanners. I expect the other inmates are grabbing whatever they can find to do the same—the smart ones, anyway. Let's go. It should be pretty obvious once we get out there whether the pacification systems are still working or not."

Ryder wrapped the fabric around the tattoo and tied it off with her teeth. The chains hanging from her wrists were seriously irritating, but she supposed they might come in useful as a makeshift weapon in a fight.

"Ready," she said, and the two women moved cautiously into the corridor outside the visiting room. The fighting hadn't reached them yet, even though they were near the entrance used by visitors. Most of the inmates were probably heading for the same doors they had arrived through for processing, rather than risk getting lost in unfamiliar areas.

They didn't have to go far before it became obvious that the pacification systems were in the same condition as the electronic door locks. The more she saw, the more Ryder thought she recognized Ash's signature all over this. Whether she would need to thank him or thump him upside the head for it remained to be seen. A random blaster beam whizzed past them, and both women flattened themselves against the wall.

Or haunt him, Ryder thought. *Haunting is also a definite possibility at this point.*

"And this prisoner is *very* important, you say?" Veila'ana asked.

"Yes," Ryder said on a sigh.

"Just checking," said her companion.

They kept low and close to the corridor wall, the crouched position reminding Ryder pointedly about the state of her bruised ribs. When they finally emerged into the open space of the Vithii women's cellblock, it was obvious that a full-scale prison riot was in progress. Guards and prisoners faced off across the area, and some of the prisoners were armed. It seemed clear that the guards would soon be overrun, based on the sheer weight of prisoner numbers.

"We'll have to get around them somehow," Ryder said. "The prisoners are going to win this one. Let's try to slip past by going behind the main mass of them."

Veila'ana paused for only an instant before saying, "Agreed. You should play captor on this one, I think."

She passed the pistol to Ryder, grip first, and Ryder wondered once again what the woman's game really was. She took the pistol, though, being critically short in the ally department at the moment. Veila'ana mussed her pale hair. Then she dragged her suit jacket off and pulled the collar of her shirt into disarray, un-tucking it partway from her tailored trousers.

Ryder grabbed her by the scruff of her neck and frog-marched her around the perimeter of the open space, keeping to the inmate's territory. Several frightened, angry, and desperate faces turned to look at them, but the ongoing firefight was a more immediate threat. As Ryder had hoped, only a couple of people tried to stop them. One of them backed up when Ryder snarled in her face, and she stunned the other one.

"This won't work in the human-controlled areas," she said in a low voice as they slipped free of the mob and headed down a new corridor. "They'll go for both of us."

"I'm well aware, believe me," Veila'ana replied in a dry tone. "Ideas?"

A beam hit the Vitharan in the shoulder and she spun around, slamming into the wall and falling to the ground.

"*Shit!*" Ryder hissed and returned fire. The shooter—a human—grunted and collapsed. Ryder dived for Veila'ana, pressing fingers to her neck. A wisp of smoke was rising from her shoulder. It hadn't been a stun beam, but it had hit high in a non-fatal area. Her vitals were steady, but a hard lump and a trickle of blood at the back of her skull proclaimed the reason behind her unconsciousness.

Pounding footsteps approached, and Ryder whirled, pistol raised, to see several humans rushing toward them, some armed with lengths of metal pipe. She fired in rapid succession, taking out three, but two more were almost on her. Springing to her feet, Ryder swung her left wrist, sending the hanging length of chain sharply across the face of the first man. The second grabbed her, but before she could try to break his hold, something heavy slammed into him.

She jerked free as he went down, narrowly managing to keep her feet. Two figures rolled across the gritty floor, grappling for position. With a jolt, Ryder recognized dark skin and dreadlocks. She lunged for the laser pistol and came up with it, balanced on one knee.

"Temple!" she snapped. "*Clear!*"

Temple snuck in a dirty uppercut and scrambled free, at which point Ryder shot his opponent and looked around a bit frantically for other threats. Nothing else was coming at them for the moment.

"Hey there, Red," Temple said a bit breathlessly, lying spread-eagled next to the stunned inmate. "Hoped I might find you around here somewhere. Who's your friend?"

He craned his neck up, clearly recognizing Veila'ana from the previous day. "Oh, shit. Dead?"

"No. Concussion, I think… along with a shoulder wound."

Temple rolled upright with a groan. He'd clearly been through the wars, and Ryder's gaze was again drawn to that nagging wound marring the lines of his well-muscled human chest.

"She on our side or theirs?" he asked, looking down at the ambassador.

"Ours as far as I can tell," Ryder told him.

"Damn," he said. "So we have to take her with us, then?" Without waiting for an answer, he reached down to pick her up, only to pause. "Spinal injury?"

"Let's hope not," Ryder said.

He nodded and lifted her into a fireman's carry with an ease that not many humans would have been able to manage with a Vitharan—even a slender one. "So… plan?"

"It's a thing in progress." She took a deep breath, trying to get her bearings and kick her brain into gear. "Here—I think we can get to the infirmary from here. If it hasn't been ransacked already, I can treat Veila'ana enough to stabilize her. From there, we'll have access to the administrative wing. What do you want to bet most of the security from that side has been called in to deal with this shit show?"

"That works for me," Temple said. "Lead the way, but talk while you're doing it. How do you know Skye? And do you have any news about Zarian or Stella?"

Ryder handed him one of the metal pipes that had fallen to the ground when she stunned the humans. She wasn't stalling, exactly, but…

"Skye is fine, or at least she was as of a couple of days ago when I last checked in," she said, ensuring that the way was clear and making her way toward a side corridor that led toward the storage areas and the infirmary. After a pause, she added, "Dr. Chantrell is dead."

Temple was silent for a long moment, though his stride didn't falter.

"I'd figured he probably was," he said eventually. "And his wife?"

"We'd hoped she was being held here as well, but she's not, according to the records. I had computer access and was able to confirm that before they nabbed me."

Temple shifted Veila'ana's unconscious body into a more comfortable position. "So you really were here for me? I wasn't sure, but it did seem like a hell of a coincidence otherwise."

"Yes," Ryder admitted. "Though as rescues go, I'm afraid it's a bit underwhelming. Honestly, I was just here for recon. I expect this fucking mess we're in now is my colleagues' idea of an escape plan."

Temple nodded. "Well, it's original if nothing else, I suppose." He tensed. "Heads up."

Ryder was already turning to follow his gaze. A human woman froze in the corridor ahead of them. She appeared to be unarmed, her smock torn and hanging off one shoulder. Holding the pistol ready but not aiming it, Ryder said, "We're no danger to you. If you can get to the admin wing, you'll be able to follow the signs to one of the exits. But if you make an aggressive move toward us, I'll stun you."

"Go on," Temple said. "You might as well beat the rush."

The woman stared at them with wide eyes for a couple of beats, then turned and ran off.

"Regime forces will be massing outside before long," he said after the woman had gone. "Getting out is only part of it."

"Yes. But it's still the first part," Ryder pointed out.

"True," he agreed, as they started moving again.

Before long, they arrived at the infirmary. Like everything else, it was unlocked, the door ajar but not gaping. Ryder shouldered it open and held it so Temple could maneuver his unconscious burden inside. She waved him to a diagnostic cot, and he lowered Veila'ana carefully onto it. The ambassador groaned as he eased her head down to the pillow.

Ryder put the pistol down on the edge of the cot and peeled back one of her eyelids, pleased to see that she was coming around. "That's a good sign," she observed.

A low laugh from the other side of the room made Ryder straighten abruptly, a chill skittering up her spine. Her hand inched toward the weapon, only to freeze when a voice said, "Don't. I have a blaster pointed at your head, pet. Turn around slowly."

With a sinking sense of inevitability, Ryder slowly turned to face the figure that had spoken.

"I thought you might come back here if you managed to avoid getting mowed down in the crossfire on the prisoner levels," Jodor said with obvious satisfaction. "You know, I don't really think anyone would question it if a respected government official were forced to shoot an escaped fugitive or two in the pursuit of his own safety during a prison riot. Do you?"

NINE

Draven was starting to second-guess his brilliant plan of popping into the middle of the prison riot, finding Ryder and Skye's brother, and popping back out again. Somehow, a thousand prisoners didn't sound like an unmanageable number to search through until you encountered them roaming around in mobs, throwing things and shooting at people.

Especially since he had a growing suspicion that Ryder might be long gone already, leaving him wandering around inside the prison like an idiot. She was smart, and she had good instincts. She would have made for an exit as soon as she realized what was going on, probably.

Just in case, he'd swung by the infirmary earlier before continuing on to the cellblocks, hoping she might have headed there. It had been deserted, however, and he guessed whatever staff was on duty had scarpered as soon as the prisoners started spilling out of their cells.

After that, he headed for the central cellblock where the humans were held, thinking she might have gone looking for their original target. Whether she had or she hadn't, the area was in chaos. Several knots of people were fighting and there was no overall strategy apparent. With three disparate groups that all hated each other—the humans, the

Vithii prisoners, and the Vithii guards—it had more or less turned into a free-for-all.

Draven craned his head, looking around for a shock of red hair, but without a view from higher ground, it was hopeless. A Vithii man charged at him, going for his stolen blaster, and Draven channeled some of his frustration into tossing the would-be attacker over his shoulder, into the wall behind him.

Disheartened and hoping desperately that Ryder was, indeed, already outside of the prison's walls and heading to safety, he made his way along the edges of the violent mob, heading for the admin wing again. He still had his maintenance tech uniform and forged identichip, meaning that it would be easy enough to stumble out of the employee entrance with the other fleeing workers.

Dressed as he was, he'd only garner a cursory security check, if that. Regime forces waiting outside wouldn't have time or resources to waste on people who appeared to be no threat. Not when they had a thousand dangerous criminals trying to break out into the city—many of whom were now armed.

A flash of colorful hair caught his eye, but an instant later he saw that it was human orange, not vibrant red. Two Vithii men and a Vithii woman had a skinny human teenage boy surrounded. The kid looked terrified, and he had one arm clamped around his stomach. Startlingly bright human blood trickled down his pale skin, staining the top of his baggy, drawstring prison shorts.

Draven wavered for a moment, knowing he couldn't really afford the time for this. The human was just a kid, though, and Draven knew the feeling of being surrounded by people who could and would pound you into the dirt for no other reason than they wanted to.

"Oy!" he called, striding over. "Get off him. He's not a threat—concentrate on the guards!"

"Fuck off!" said the taller of the two men. "He's human scum. His kind's the reason we're in this mess to start with. Fuckin' parasites!"

Draven wasted only a second trying to follow the man's reasoning. Shaking his head to try to dissipate the miasma of *stupid* that was hovering over the little group, he sighed and stunned all three in quick succession.

"C'mon, kid," he told the boy, who had stumbled backward as his tormenters fell to the ground. "How bad did they get you? Can you walk?"

He eyed the human, whose slate-blue eyes were wide and terrified.

"I… I think so," he stammered.

"Good. What's your name? I'm Draven." He swept an eye over their surroundings, splitting his attention between trying to reassure the kid and making sure they weren't about to get jumped on or shot.

"It's uh, Jonah." His eyes narrowed. "Why are you helping me?"

"Why wouldn't I help you?" Draven shot back with some asperity. "Now, let's go. I'm heading for the employee exit in the administration wing. There are some unconscious employees back there. We'll take their clothes off them and dress you up like a civvy so you can come out with me. Quick, lemme see that wound in your gut."

Jonah looked like he was torn between believing this was all some kind of trick, and thanking the prophets for his good fortune. He peeled his blood-soaked arm away, and Draven glanced at the wound.

"It's not spurting, and nothing inside is falling out," he reported. "I expect it'll keep for a bit. Now, *move.*"

With that, he grabbed the human's arm and headed once more toward the admin wing, scanning their surroundings for threats. A full-strength blaster beam took a chunk out of the wall a meter or so above their heads, and Jonah flinched violently. Draven gritted his teeth and kept going.

Fifteen minutes later, they were out of the dingy metal-and-plasticrete prison area and back in the carpeted beige hallways. There were only a handful of prisoners here, and no one seemed interested in accosting them. Draven figured these were the smart inmates, who were more interested in getting out safely than in bashing heads.

Draven herded Jonah to the server room where the stunned employees from earlier would hopefully provide some clothes for a disguise. As he had half-suspected, more techs had already been called in to try to fix the security system. He stunned them, noticing the light on the blaster flashing purple as the last one fell. *Battery warning.*

Oh, well, he thought. Hopefully, he wouldn't have much further use for it anyway.

He looked around and located the smallest of the Vithii women in the room. The clothing would still hang on Jonah's skinny human frame, but at least it was unisex. He started pulling off her shoes and tailored trousers, tossing them at Jonah.

"Put these on. Don't take too long," he ordered.

Grabbing a shirt from one of the men, he ripped the sleeves off and tied them together, then balled up the remainder and pressed it against Jonah's wound as the boy hissed in pain.

"Sorry, kid," he said, tying it into place with the torn sleeves. "It has to be tight to slow the blood flow."

"I know," Jonah ground out, his jaw clenching. "Give me a shirt to wear so we can get out of here."

Draven helped him into the woman's shirt and he fastened it partway up the front. They left the server room and headed for the entrance.

"If security tries to hassle you, tell them you're one of the sub-intendants' administrative assistants, and that you lost your identichip when an inmate attacked you. Hopefully they'll be in too much of a rush to check you for a prisoner tattoo if you look harmless."

"Yeah, okay," Jonah said.

Draven steadied him with a grip on the arm that wasn't pressing the balled-up shirt against his stomach, and led him down the stairwell to the ground floor. They followed the signs to the exit. Before they hit the last turning, Draven pulled the power cell from the blaster and tossed it in one room, then threw the blaster itself in another.

"Remember, we're just harmless, unarmed workers who got caught up in this shit," he said. "Nothing dangerous or interesting about us. We're simply part of the collateral damage."

Raising his free hand and keeping the one on Jonah's arm in plain sight, Draven led them out the door. "We're employees!" he shouted. "Tell us what to do! Can we come out?"

"Keep your hands where we can see them!" called one of the armed Regime guards. "Step forward!"

"This guy's injured, okay?" Draven said, nudging Jonah to put his hands up.

"Step forward!" The guard repeated.

"It'll be all right," he muttered to the kid, too low for the guards to hear.

They walked forward, stopping a few paces in front of the line of security forces. The one who had spoken came up to stand before them, his hand resting on his sidearm but not drawing it. With all the guns pointed at them from the line of guards, he hardly needed to.

"I'm a contractor. I have an identichip," Draven said, not moving his hands. "It's in my right trouser pocket."

"Hand it over slowly," said the Regime guard. "No sudden moves."

Draven did, and the man pulled a scanner from his belt. He ran it over the chip and gave a cursory glance at the results before nodding.

"Right, you can go." His eyes fell on Jonah and narrowed. "Human, eh? You work in there?" He jerked his chin at the prison.

"I'm Sub-Intendant Cheraat's secretary," Jonah said, not looking up to meet the guard's eyes. "I'm s-sorry. A couple of the human inmates got into the admin wing and attacked me. They called me a race traitor. Then they took my ID chip and smashed it."

Draven had to hand it to the kid—he was good. Calling himself a secretary rather than the snootier term 'administrative assistant'; making his attackers out to be humans rather than Vithii. Playing into the guards' preconceived stereotypes.

"I'll vouch for him. I saw him hanging around the break room this morning when I came in," Draven said. "Look, I don't think they knew exactly where to find the exit, but there were at least a couple of dozen inmates heading in this general direction when we snuck out. Can we get out of here before they show up and the shooting starts?"

The guard's features hardened at the mention of inmates. "Yeah, fine. I'll authorize it. Vacate the immediate area. You said this one was injured?" His eyes flicked to Jonah.

"Don't worry, I'll get him to a clinic or something," Draven said. "We're good now. Just point us in the direction we should go."

***

Ryder stared at the blaster muzzle pointing at her head, and at the man behind it. A man she'd once thought she knew as well as she knew herself.

"Finally mustered the courage to do the job yourself, rather than hiring it out?" she asked, resignation coloring her tone.

"Step away from the cot," Jodor said, not rising to the taunt.

Ryder wondered if he was more worried about her going for the laser pistol, or about accidentally hitting the ambassador when he shot her. She did as he'd ordered, moving slowly, aware that Temple had remained where he was. She didn't react, resisting the urge to meet the human's eyes. Temple still had the metal pipe, held casually next his leg.

Jodor didn't have military or fighting experience. He'd been a paper-pusher his entire adult life. He was focused on Ryder—not worrying about the tactical mistake of trying to cover two people with one weapon when they weren't standing right next to each other. She kept stepping around the room, doing exactly as he'd asked, waiting for the moment he realized his mistake and hoping Temple was thinking what she thought he was thinking.

Sure enough, Jodor's eyes flickered back toward the cot. "Stop! That's far enough." The blaster's aim wavered as he was caught in a moment's indecision about where to point it.

"Down!" Temple snapped, exploding into motion. Ryder dove for the floor, seeing Temple hurl the heavy pipe at Jodor's weapon in a shining arc. The pipe hit his arm and the blaster went off, the wild shot missing both of them. Temple lunged for Jodor, while Ryder lunged for the laser pistol on the edge of the cot.

The human and Vithii males crashed together. Ryder gathered Temple had managed to hold his own against a couple of Vithii in the exercise yard before someone had stabbed him, but those had been prisoners—starved and confined for who knew how long. Weakened.

Jodor was not a trained fighter, but he was large even for a Vithii, towering over Temple despite the human's nearly two-meter height. He was also rested, well fed, uninjured, and sporting the bulging musculature he'd faithfully maintained with a gym membership since before Ryder first met him. Temple barely stood a chance. Ryder tried to get a clear shot as they grappled and traded blows.

The human was fighting dirty, but his jabs and kicks only seemed to enrage Jodor further.

She couldn't hit one without hitting both, and she couldn't afford for Temple to be out of commission from a stun beam if they were going to get out of here before the Regime forces arrived to lock the place down.

Inevitably, Jodor found an opening and hit Temple with a blow that drove him to the ground, where he lay unmoving. Jodor whirled on Ryder and she took her shot, aiming for the center of his chest. The pistol heated in her hand and a weak beam emerged, staggering Jodor back a step, but not felling him.

Out of power.

Jodor bared his teeth in a rictus of a grin that was almost a snarl. He stepped over Temple's body and crouched, picking up the blaster before stalking toward Ryder with murder in his eyes. She backed up, eyes flashing around the room for anything that might be useful as a weapon, but everything had been properly secured and stowed before the staff had evacuated.

"Your sins have haunted me for long enough, Lyn," he said, coming to a stop a few steps away, next to the cot. He raised the blaster, pointing it at her forehead, and Ryder closed her eyes, defeated.

I'm sorry, she thought to all the people she'd let down. Temple. Skye. Hunter.

Her son.

She waited for fiery pain, followed by oblivion, but instead, a sharp grunt came from the man in front of her. Ryder's eyes flew open to see Veila'ana sitting up on the cot, her fingers pressed to the side of Jodor's face. His expression morphed into slack shock, and the blaster slipped from his nerveless fingers to fall to the ground. His body followed a moment later.

"... what?" Ryder asked faintly.

Veila'ana watched him closely for a moment, and then straightened to stare at Ryder with her disconcerting pale gaze. "He's very tired," she said. "He needed to sleep for a bit."

Ryder blinked, trying to reboot her brain and twist the facts to fit around what she'd just seen. Her attention fell on the ambassador's hair—such a light shade of platinum, it was nearly white. It... *could* have come from a bottle. Or...

"You're not Vitharan," she said.

Veila'ana raised a pale blonde eyebrow. "Of course I'm Vitharan." A faint smile tugged at one corner of her wide mouth, slow and dangerous. "On my father's side."

Ah. "And on your mother's side?" she asked.

"Maelfian," Veila'ana said easily.

A telepath. That made sense. *Holy shit.*

"And who are you, really?" Ryder pressed. "What are you doing here? Why are you helping me?"

"I really am a Vitharan ambassador, here to observe the Ilarian criminal justice system," Veila'ana said with every appearance of truthfulness. "And why wouldn't I help you? Your bondmate was just about to murder you in cold blood."

Ryder shook her head. "No. No, that's not good enough. You asked if I was guilty of the charges against me and I told you I was. But you were all ready to help me escape."

Veila'ana didn't answer. Instead, she took a breath and rotated her shoulder as if testing it—the same shoulder that had taken a glancing hit from a blaster set on full. Ryder's eyes fell to the scorched hole in her sleeve. "Let me check Temple's vitals and I'll treat that for you."

The other woman only waved her off. "No need. Maelfians heal rather efficiently, thanks to the ability to channel mental power into physical regeneration. Don't worry about it. Focus on your human; you still need to get him out of here."

Ryder stopped herself from saying *he's not my human*, knowing there was no time to waste. Instead, she nodded. Temple still lay unmoving on the floor. Crouching next to him, Ryder saw a vivid bruise blossoming across his jaw. Fortunately, it didn't seem to be broken, and his pupils reacted almost normally when she peeled his eyelids up. She crossed to a storage cabinet, hoping they hadn't thought to change the codes on the locks after she'd been arrested.

It turned out to be a moot point. The electronic locks on the cabinets were open just like every other lock in the prison complex. She fished out a mediscanner and returned to her patient, running it over his skull. As she'd suspected, Temple had a mild concussion, but seemed unharmed otherwise. She rolled him onto his back and gave into the urge to grab a protoplaser so she could finally finish closing up the damned knife slash from the other day.

It was a mess, having been reopened multiple times and now showing signs of infection. Even so, a few minutes' work and another hypo injector of broad-spectrum antibiotic completed the job that should have been done when it was fresh.

It would probably scar, and she wondered if he would care. Looking down at his attractive human face, solemn and serious even in unconsciousness, she somehow doubted it. A second hypo, this one with a stimulant, had him groaning and coming around almost immediately.

"Son of a bitch," he slurred, "what just hit me?"

With no more patients to focus on, reaction was setting in, but Ryder still forced herself to quip, "My ex, as it happens. Don't worry, Veila'ana and I took care of him for you."

Temple's eyes sharpened, his awareness of their situation returning as Ryder watched. "Right. He's out of the equation, then? Did you kill him?"

The question sparked Ryder's tangled swirl of hatred and biological need, so she was relieved when Veila'ana answered for her.

"No. He's just settling in for a little nap. He won't be going anywhere for a few hours." She frowned. "You two need to move. Regime forces will have arrived by now. Ryder, I'd hoped to be able to sneak you out one of the admin or visitors' entrances, but by now I suspect they'll be shooting first and asking questions later."

Ryder thought furiously. If the Regime really was camped out around the prison, their only chance at this point might be to join the main mass of inmates trying to force their way out through the prisoners' entrance, and hope for the best.

"We can't stay here," Temple said, echoing her thoughts. "You can, though—and in fact, you probably should. You're a diplomat, right? If you hole up somewhere defensible, will you be all right here until things are under control again?"

"Probably," said Veila'ana. "Though I don't like the idea of you two walking into a war zone to try to get out. I'm sorry I slowed you down. Should've ducked faster, I guess."

Ryder was still running through possible scenarios when a thought hit her. "Oh!" she exclaimed, snapping her fingers. "Scrubs!"

Temple peered at her in confusion. "Excuse me?"

"Scrubs," she repeated, rummaging through a different storage cabinet and coming up with a couple sets of medical scrubs in a cheerful blue color. She tossed one set to Temple. "Quick, put these on."

Understanding dawned on the human's face. "Ah. Smart," he approved. He turned his back and efficiently stripped off the torn prison pants that were all he'd been wearing. For an instant, Ryder was staring at a sleek back and a set of well-muscled glutes, before she caught herself and focused on her own clothing.

Veila'ana gave her a critical once over after she pulled a lab coat out of a closet to complete the ensemble. "I wouldn't put it past your bondmate to have put out a description of you to the authorities," she said. "Is there anything here you can use to cover up your hair? It's a bit... distinctive."

You're one to talk, Ryder thought, but didn't say. "Fair point," she allowed, and rummaged around for a square of cotton bandaging cloth that she could use to fashion a headscarf. "Right. Temple, you're an orderly. They don't actually have any human nurses or orderlies in this prison, but the security forces probably won't know that. No way they'd buy you being a doctor here, though."

He nodded, but his expression was tense. "If they think to check our forearms for a barcode, we're screwed."

"That's why we're taking our chances with the prisoner mob at the main inmate processing entrance," she told him. "Banking on people's innate respect for the medical profession to keep them from purposely blowing our heads off."

He blinked at her. "And what keeps them from accidentally blowing our heads off?"

She grinned, showing teeth. "Not a damned thing."

TEN

The guard outside the employee entrance directed Draven to a staging area two blocks west, which Draven had no intention of getting anywhere near. Instead, he led Jonah past the line of guns and hard faces, and didn't stop until they were a couple of streets away. Jonah collapsed against the wall of a building, shaking.

"Holy fuck," he said. "We did it. We *did* it."

He flashed the human a quick, sharp grin. "Told you it'd be fine."

Jonah laughed, a bit hysterically, only to grunt and double over as the movement jarred his side.

Draven waited until he recovered enough to straighten up before telling him, "You did good. Don't think I didn't notice how you played along with the guard's anti-human sentiments, and made him discount you as a threat. Now. You got anyplace to go?"

Jonah's face went through a complex series of expressions, ending with wariness. "Yeah... I mean, I guess so. I've got a gang I can go back to, unless the security forces managed to round all of them up. I saw a few back in the prison."

It's odd to look at a gawky human kid with orange hair and see a reflection of yourself, Draven thought.

Shit. The timing here was not good, but he wasn't about to send a teenager off to a gang that might or might not still exist—with no money, no ID, and an untreated knife wound.

"You should get that wound seen to sooner rather than later," he said. "You can come with me if you want, and find your gang once the fuss dies down a bit."

Jonah stared at him. "What's your angle?"

Draven shrugged. "I was like you, once. I remember what it can be like. I've got friends nearby, so I'm offering."

He watched as Jonah visibly wavered, probably fighting years of indoctrination into hating—and being hated by—Vithii. But the kid was smart. Draven wasn't surprised when he finally gave a tight nod. "Okay. Thanks. I probably wouldn't have gotten out of there in one piece if you hadn't helped me."

"It wasn't a big deal," Draven said. "Now, come on. I want to get off the streets before things get any crazier."

He led the boy a block north and two blocks east, bringing them one street over from the road that bounded the west side of the prison complex. He was still hoping that Ryder had made it out of one of the admin wing entrances and he'd just missed her. Pax had one of those entrances under surveillance and Ash had the other. Ash would probably terrify Jonah less, but Pax's location was closer. The cyborg also had more training in field medicine.

And you don't trust yourself to be alone with Ash these days if you can possibly avoid it, goaded a little voice in the back of Draven's head, which he studiously ignored.

"One of my friends is hiding out in this building, watching the prison," he said. "You're gonna want to freak out when you see him. Do us both a favor, and don't. He's all right, no matter what kind of shit you've seen on the newsvids. Okay?"

"Uh… okay?" Jonah said.

Draven made his way into the alley next to the building, which was some kind of rent-an-office place with, Kade assured them, a high vacancy rate and low standards for tenancy. Pax was staking out the prison from an office on the fourth floor, giving him an excellent bird's-eye view of the entrance Draven and Jonah had just come from.

They took the lift to save Jonah having to jog up four flights of stairs with his side still bleeding, and Draven led him to the right suite number. He knocked on the door in a complicated code. It opened a moment later to reveal Pax's imposing figure. The cyborg's face was hidden in the shadow of a hooded jacket, and he held a laser pistol casually in one huge hand. Next to Draven, Jonah took an unsteady step away from the huge, armed Vithii. Draven snaked out an arm and dragged him forward again.

"I did warn you, kid," he said, even though the real freak-out situation was probably yet to come, once the human saw the implants molded to the side of Pax's face.

"Picking up strays, Draven?" Pax asked. "I saw you both come out together earlier."

Draven ignored the question. "Let us in and close the door, Pax. The kid's hurt, and I want to hear the latest. Any eyes on Ryder yet?"

Pax let them slide past, into the sparsely furnished space beyond. Jonah stuck close to the door, eyes darting nervously between the two.

"Nothing so far," Pax said, and Draven's heart sank.

"Who's Ryder?" Jonah asked. "One of your co-workers?" He indicated Draven's maintenance tech uniform with one hand.

"Yes and no," Draven said, not quite ready to start spouting sensitive details to the kid, even if he did like him.

"Her hair should make her relatively easy to pick out, even in a crowd," Pax said, "but there were no sightings as of the last check-in five minutes ago."

"*Shite*," Draven cursed.

"Hang on," Jonah said tentatively. "Back up for a minute. What about her hair?"

"It's red," Draven said shortly.

Jonah frowned. "You mean like mine?"

"No," Draven clarified "it's... *red*."

There was a pause, and Jonah said, "Oh, hell. And she's Vithii, right?"

Immediately, he was the center of attention, and he flinched back a bit from the intense regard. His mouth opened, but nothing came out.

Draven narrowly stopped himself from barging forward and grabbing the kid. "You saw her? *When*?"

"Y-yesterday," he stammered. "But... the woman I saw was a prisoner, not an employee. The guards threw her in with a bunch of us. Human guys, I mean. They place bets on shit like that when the supervisors aren't paying attention. She, uh, she said she was a doctor or something."

Draven growled, his fists balling up at his sides, and Jonah squeezed back a little harder against the door.

"He's not snarling at you," Pax said in that flat voice of his. "Not unless you were responsible for any harm coming to Ryder, at any rate."

"No!" Jonah said, sounding so appalled that Draven immediately believed him. "She's okay. Or, I mean, she was okay when they came and took her out of the exercise yard yesterday. She brawled with a couple of the guys, but me and a friend of mine stood up for her and it didn't go very far. Then, some Vithii suits showed up, and so did the prison Intendant. They got her out, and one of them said something about getting her legal counsel. That's all I know, man!"

Draven made himself relax. "We were right, then. She's still an inmate."

"It was always the most likely scenario," Pax pointed out, and at times like this, Draven envied him his lack of emotion.

He turned to Jonah. "It was good of you to stand up for her. Not many would."

Jonah suddenly looked uncomfortable, as though he were unaccustomed to praise. "Well, it was mostly Temple, really. He jumped in as soon as some of the others started in on her."

Draven frowned and shot a look of incredulity at Pax. "Temple?" he asked Jonah slowly. "Temple Akenzua?"

Jonah blinked at him a few times. "Uh… maybe? I don't know his last name. Tall guy, dreadlocks. Mixed race, black and Asian?"

"Oh, you have got to be shitting me," Draven said.

"What? Why?" Jonah asked, obviously bewildered. "Temple used to be a courier and a fixer for some of the gangs. He helped me out once or twice, that's all. I didn't know he was inside until they threw us into the exercise yard together."

"Well, she obviously found him," Pax observed. "After a fashion."

Draven dragged a hand through his hair and started pacing. "She probably went back to try and get him when the security went down. Fuck. *Fuck*."

Pax watched him, unmoving. "It changes nothing. If she succeeds, all the better." His eyes settled on Jonah again. "You're bleeding on the carpet. We'll lose the deposit."

Jonah looked down, and his cheeks colored. "Er, sorry…?"

Pax shook his head beneath the shadow of his hood, obviously approaching capacity when it came to dealing with meatbags. "Come," he said. "I brought a medikit in case there were injuries. I might not be Ryder, but I can at least patch you up while we wait for news."

━━━━◆━━━━

Temple was giving Ryder the kind of look people gave you when they thought you had mental issues, but he only said, "So, our plan is to walk into a mob full of people shooting at each other? Super. I can hardly wait. Are we ready to go, then?"

Veila'ana tossed Ryder the blaster that had fallen from Jodor's slack fingers. "You need it more than I do," said the Vitharan.

Ryder looked at the deadly weapon in her hand, and then she looked at the man lying on the floor, soft snores emerging from his throat. It would be so easy…

Temple was watching her with complete understanding. "I wouldn't blame you a damned bit if you did it," he said softly.

She ground her jaw, conflicting impulses fighting for dominance. "No," she said finally, unwilling to be the woman who killed both her bondmate and her child. "Come on. Let's go."

"Good luck," Veila'ana told her. "Oh! Just a second." She grabbed a pen and a slip of paper from one of the counters along the wall and jotted something down. "This comm code is untraceable, but if you send a message to it, I'll get it within a day or so. Who knows? It might come in handy sometime."

Ryder took it and slipped it into the pocket of the borrowed scrubs. "Thank you. Not just for this, but—" She gestured at Jodor. "You know. Everything."

"Don't mention it," the other woman said wryly. "And I do mean that. *Don't mention it*—at least, not to anyone you don't trust with your life."

Ryder nodded, and she and Temple headed out in the direction of the inmate levels. Temple gestured at the lengths of chain dangling from Ryder's wrists. "You might want to wrap those up and hide them under your sleeves," he suggested. "Bit of a giveaway otherwise."

Ryder felt a faint, uncharacteristic flush rise to her cheeks. "Just making sure you were paying attention," she said, and wrapped the chains around her forearms, tucking the ends under to keep them in place and tugging her sleeves down over them.

The throng of inmates had gained more of a united sense of purpose than it had exhibited earlier. Evidently, for most of the prisoners, the desire to get out had overwhelmed the desire to brawl with anyone who didn't look like them. Hundreds of them now pressed toward the entrance where new prisoners were brought in for processing. The shooting inside the prison had died down to almost nothing, which told Ryder that the guards had finally been overcome, leaving no appreciable resistance inside the walls.

Outside the walls, it would be a very different thing, however. She wondered idly if the Regime security forces had orders to stun or to kill. Had the escapees all been human, she would have put money on them simply mowing down every person that made it through the doors. The presence of both Vithii and humans muddied the waters, though, especially since Ryder knew now that there were diplomatic observers from Vithara—and possibly other members of the Seven Systems—in the political mix.

Somewhat to her surprise, a warm hand took her own. Temple twined their fingers together and squeezed. "Here goes nothing," he said, as they made for the fringes of the mob.

Ryder tried not to be distracted by the feeling of his hand in hers. For eight years, she had barely touched anyone outside of a medical treatment setting, and hardly anyone had touched her. Honestly, the only person she could think of that didn't avoid the touch of her skin like the plague was Ash, who seemed to think nothing of giving her shoulder an occasional squeeze or her back a quick pat.

But Ash was a) human, b) homosexual, and c) mad as a box of hats. For some reason, the idea of Temple wrapping her hand up in his was disconcerting in a way that Ash's casual lack of boundaries… wasn't. It was disconcerting in the same way it had been disconcerting to realize earlier that she was staring at his naked ass while her traitorous bondmate lay unconscious on the floor only a few meters away.

And this was decidedly *not* the time to be worrying about it, as something solid flew past her head and crashed into a wall nearby. Prophets, anyone would think *she* was the one with the concussion. At least Temple had an excuse for acting strangely. His hand tightened on hers, and she let him lead her toward a place where the crowd wasn't pressed together quite so tightly.

It was the moment when they would have to let themselves be surrounded as they tried to get lost in the central mass, and slip free when they were outside. Once in the security forces' sights, they'd be relying entirely on their disguises as medical personnel to keep them alive as they broke through the Regime lines to get to freedom.

It was a shit strategy, Ryder knew. If it went bad, she planned on blaming whichever of her comrades had originally come up with the prison riot idea, because that was also a shit strategy.

This is what happens when you volunteer for things, she thought. *Every soldier and every first-year medical resident knows that. What's your excuse, you idiot?*

The roar of people yelling and the sound of weapons fire ahead of them grew so loud that there was no hope of communicating at a normal volume.

Fortunately, while the plan was shit, it was also straightforward—get out the door without getting killed, ditch the blaster before the security forces saw it, stick their hands up in the air, and make a run for it.

Unfortunately, as they got farther into the heart of the mob and closer to the door, the press of bodies got tighter and the jostling grew more violent. Ryder didn't want to use the blaster—even on the stun setting—for fear that doing so would set off a stampede and get them or other people trampled to death. She found herself clinging to Temple's hand like a lifeline, desperate not to get separated from him.

They were almost to the entrance when someone slammed against Ryder's back so violently that she felt the snap as one of her bruised ribs gave way. She gasped, staggering, the intake of breath igniting fire in the left side of her chest. Temple's grip kept her from going down under the press of bodies, but then a hoarse human voice screamed, "Fucking Vithii bitch!" and sharp agony flared as a blade slid into her shoulder from behind.

ELEVEN

Temple felt Red lurch beside him. He whirled, the sudden movement making it feel like his brain was sloshing around inside his injured head. The short, stout human man who had been one of the ringleaders in the exercise yard stood there with a shiv clutched in his hand. He was pressed in close, hemmed in place by the crowd around them. Temple saw copper-colored Vithii blood dripping from the makeshift blade and cursed.

He grabbed the man's wrist and twisted, digging his thumb in until the shiv clattered to the plasticrete floor, and immediately kicking it out of reach. He wanted to ram a fist into the guy's nose, but if the violence drew in more people and spiraled out of control, they were screwed. Instead, he scooped the blaster from Red's slackening grip and pointed in the guy's face in clear warning. *Back off, or you're going down.*

The hatred on that face was startling in its intensity. For a moment, Temple thought he'd call the bluff. After a tense frozen moment, though, he snarled something Temple couldn't hear and disappeared into the crowd.

He and Red were still being pressed along with the mob, getting closer to the doors and the sound of fighting beyond. Temple dragged Red's arm over his shoulder and wrapped the arm holding the blaster around her middle to keep her upright.

Warm wetness trickled down to coat his forearm. He didn't know exactly where the wound was. He also didn't know how bad it was, and he couldn't stop and check with the crowd surging around them.

All he could do was keep them on their feet and moving forward.

He shot a sideways glance at Red's face, which was set tight in lines of pain. She was moving, though, even if her weight leaned heavily on him. Temple was tall for a human and Red was average for a Vithii woman, putting them on a fairly even footing. Her large brown eyes flickered to his, and she jerked her chin forward in clear instruction.

Keep going.

He tried not to think about the fact that this wasn't even the dangerous part. The dangerous part was yet to come. He knew, though, that any chance of escape was better than remaining in this stinking prison where he could be used as a pawn against Skye. Given the choice between a painful and messy death at the wrong end of a blaster beam, versus being in any way responsible for Skye being captured or killed, Temple would take his chances with the afterlife.

Ahead of them, the inmates were packed so tightly they could barely breathe as they squeezed through the bottleneck of the entrance and into the warzone beyond. A shocking number were armed with energy weapons—there must not be a single prison guard still standing behind them.

He looked around, searching out a likely candidate to give their blaster to once they got to the doors. More covering fire coming from the inmate side could only help them, but Red had been right.

If they emerged into the Regime forces' blaster sights while brandishing a weapon, they'd become an instant target, medical scrubs or no. Especially if he—a human—emerged brandishing a weapon. He had no illusions about how much value the security forces outside would place on his life, regardless of what kind of clothes he was wearing.

A sharp-faced Vithii woman in a prisoner smock was pressing against his left side. He sized her up and transferred the blaster to his left hand awkwardly, not letting go of Red as he did. Nudging the unfamiliar woman with his shoulder, he offered her the blaster grip-first when she glared at him. She pinned Temple with a distrustful look, but when he continued to hold the weapon out for her to take, she grabbed it and offered him a tight nod.

They were squished together hard as the crowd behind them pushed them through the doors. Red flinched in his supportive embrace as she was shoved and jostled. Temple gripped her tight, holding her close against his side. He still had only the vaguest idea who she was, but it was pretty clear to him that today, the two of them would either stand or fall together.

The doors disgorged them, blinking, into the light, to reveal a hellish landscape of fallen inmates and sizzling blaster beams whizzing past from both directions. They had to clamber over a growing wall of fallen bodies. Temple's gorge tried to rise as his bare feet stumbled on soft body parts. He had no idea if they were stunned or dead, and he wasn't about to look down and try to find out.

Beside him, Red staggered and nearly dragged both of them down as she tried to negotiate the uneven footing. He kept them upright by sheer force of will, knowing that if they fell, they'd be trampled just like the unlucky prisoners they were climbing over.

His feet hit bare pavement again as the crowd around them began to spread out. A human woman screamed and fell a couple of meters to his right, the smoking hole in her chest answering any question he might have had about whether the guards were using lethal force.

Fuck it, he thought. *Being killed is better than being stunned, dragged back into that damned building, and thrown into a cell again.*

"Hands up!" he tried to shout to Red, lifting his into view as best he could without dropping her.

He didn't know whether she just hadn't heard him, or whether her injury made raising her arms impossible. Whatever the case, she just continued to stagger along next to him, her arm heavy across his shoulders. He angled her toward the side of the mob, trying to separate them from the main mass of the crowd so the soldiers would be able to see their clothing—and hopefully not gun them down by accident while aiming at the prisoners.

A beam sizzled past his hip, leaving white-hot pain where it grazed him. Behind him, he heard a scream as someone less lucky went down.

"*Medics!*" he roared at the top of his lungs. "*We're medics! Let us through!*"

He continued to steer them perpendicular to the direction of the main mass of prisoners. Several more blaster beams came close, but none hit them. Before long, they were free of the crowd. The Regime forces were deployed in an arc around the entrance—hundreds of them, standing in ranks three or four deep, ready to step forward if their comrades fell and ensure that no prisoners escaped the perimeter.

Without the scrubs, they would have had no chance whatsoever. With a sinking feeling, Temple thought of Jonah, and hoped like hell that the kid was safe rather than lying at the bottom of the pile of bodies they'd just climbed over.

"We're non-combatants!" he shouted as they approached the ranks of twitchy Regime guards. "Please, don't shoot!"

The guards' faces were blank masks behind their reflective black riot helmets and visors, but the line of blaster muzzles pointing at them didn't erupt into beams of fiery death. Temple's heart was pounding like it might leap completely free of his chest as he supported Red the last few meters to the first line of soldiers, but there was no way out except forward.

At the last moment, the line gave way, the Vithii guards opening a small gap for them to slip through.

"Report to the staging area, one block east!" one of them snapped.

Temple nodded eagerly, feeling as though his neck were on a hinge, and immediately rushed for the nearest shadowed corner as soon as the security soldiers' backs were turned.

"Holy shit," he muttered as he dragged Red's slumped form toward the nearest shelter he could find. "Holy shit. Holy *shit*."

He collapsed back-first into the mouth of an alley, pulling Red around to rest against his front in what was nearly an embrace. A month ago, Temple would have told anyone who asked that he'd been in a scrape or two in his time. That was before he'd come to understand what real danger was.

Playing decoy in the heart of a Regime complex.

Walking unarmed into the middle of a prison riot.

It was a miracle he was still fucking alive.

"Red," he said, aware that his limbs were trembling like a palsy victim's. "We're clear. Talk to me."

Red was slumped against his chest, pressing against him from chest to knee. He wished right now that he was in a state to appreciate it properly, but all he felt was adrenalin crash coupled with stark fear. After a moment, she lifted her head, and he could breathe again.

"There's a rendezvous point," she said weakly. "Don't think I can make it that far, though. We have to get off the streets."

"Okay," he said, trying to think through the fog of exhaustion and relief. "Okay, we'll find someplace."

***

Ryder could feel the pulse of blood pumping out of the wound in her shoulder, the chill of encroaching shock at odds with the warmth all down her front where her body pressed against Temple's. He was shaking. Had he been injured, and she'd missed it somehow? She didn't think so.

They'd made it… after a fashion, at any rate.

She wanted nothing more than to be instantaneously transported to the rendezvous point where someone would be waiting to patch her up and whisk them away to safety. Where was Kade's matter transport unit when you really needed it? She wouldn't even complain about puking her guts out at the end of the journey.

She let Temple ease her around until he was supporting her with his shoulder again, and followed where he led. Her legs felt heavy; it was a struggle to keep putting one in front of the other. Shit, she could really use a chance to sit down, but the practical part of her knew that once she was down, she wouldn't be getting up again without some serious help.

She was vaguely aware that they were traveling through the alleys between buildings. A door creaked open on rusting hinges. The space beyond was cool and dark. She had a vague impression of shelves, counters, and the smell of stale cooking grease. Then Temple was hooking a chair away from the wall with his foot, turning it around and lowering her to straddle it backwards. She slumped forward, bracing herself on her forearms against the seatback.

"Where are we?" she asked, exhaustion making the words slur.

"Restaurant," he said. "Not sure what it's called, but I think this area must've been evacuated when the prisoners started trying to get out. Hang on, I need to find the lights and something to cut those scrubs away from your shoulder."

Ryder just wanted to sleep, but she knew it was important that she stay awake long enough to find out what state the wound was in, and to get Temple directions to the rendezvous. The lights switched on and she squinted as they stabbed into her brain. He returned a moment later.

"You think I can slide the lab coat off without cutting it?" he asked.

She grunted an affirmative and let her arms slide down to hang loose at her sides. Her right hand was numb, only a distant tingling letting her know it was still there. *Nerve damage,* she diagnosed absently. *That's going to be a rancid bitch to deal with when I can't even reach the fucking injury without help.*

Temple eased the coat off and used a kitchen knife to slice the neckline of the scrubs enough that he could spread it apart and see the wound. "It's deep, but not long," he said. "Still bleeding pretty good."

She nodded, only to wince when the movement pulled at the hole in her shoulder. "Tear some strips from the lab coat and pack it into the wound. You'll need to keep strong pressure on it for a few minutes to try and slow the bleeding. Then you can go to the rendezvous address and get help from the others."

There was a tense moment of silence. "I don't like the idea of leaving you here alone."

"And I don't like the idea of still being here when the evacuation order is lifted and the owners come back to find me bleeding out on their kitchen floor," she snapped, pain and reaction making her temper short.

"All right," Temple said after a beat. "Fair point." She heard the sound of fabric ripping, and he continued, "I think you'd better lie down for this. I know how much pressure it can take to stop a wound bleeding, and I can get better leverage if you're lying on your front."

It was a reasonable suggestion. She dragged herself out of the chair, not waving off his help when he took her arm and led her through to the seating area, which was carpeted. He eased her down and gave her a wad of rolled-up dishtowels to use as a pillow.

"You've done this before then?" she asked.

"Not on anything this serious, but… yeah." She could feel him moving around, gathering what he'd need. "I expect this part's gonna suck big time. Sorry in advance."

With that, a wad of fabric pressed into the hole in her shoulder. She clenched her jaw to hold back the scream that wanted to escape. He leaned on the wound with a good portion of his not-inconsiderable weight.

"All right?" he asked in a worried tone.

She took a few moments to try and drag her breathing back under control. Even so, her tone was reedy as she said. "Oh, yeah. *Brilliant.* I live for this kind of shit."

Temple blew out a breath. "Anything I can do to help?"

She thought about it. "Keep talking. Distract me."

He shifted his weight beside her. "Okay. Where's this meeting place I'm supposed to go to? And what will I find there when I do?"

"I had a flat rented under the fake identity when I took the job as prison doctor," Ryder said, pausing as the pain flared higher and then subsided a bit. "But we knew if anything went wrong the authorities would be all over the place. So we agreed on a second location where I'd go if things went bad. It was empty—just a room with comm equipment in it, so I could contact the others without risking anyone following me straight to their doorstep. Someone should be there now, though. They'll know it's where I'd head if I got out."

"What's the address, and is there a code or something I'll need once I get there?"

"It's not far," she said. "Maybe half a klick. It's room three-twenty-one in the *Vre'Kalsh* building, at the corner of High Street and Forty-Second Avenue. Entry code to the building is four-seven-eight-six. The door code to the room is one-nine-five-eight, but you should knock first. Three short, four long, three short."

"I'll write it down before I go," he said. "My brain is a bit of a disaster zone at the moment." He paused. "Will Skye be there?"

"Not sure," Ryder said. "They probably have eyes on all four of the prison entrances right now. I don't know who's where."

The silence stretched before Temple asked, "Were you really there to find me?"

"Yes," she said simply.

More silence.

"Then what was all that shit with your ex about? Why was he trying to have you stitched up on fake charges?"

Ryder's heart skipped and stuttered as she remembered that Jodor had blurted out the charges against her when they were standing outside the exercise yard. While Temple was only a couple of meters away, well within hearing distance. Her vision wavered as the past battered at her weakened defenses.

Unlicensed medical experimentation on a child, resulting in death.

"They aren't fake charges," she whispered.

The pressure on her back lessened, as though Temple had unconsciously shrunk away from her. An instant later, he pressed down again. She welcomed the renewed wash of physical pain, since it distracted her from the emotional pain she wasn't willing to examine right now.

"No," he said, surprising her. "I don't believe that."

She wasn't sure how to respond to his words, so she didn't. They remained in silence for several minutes before Temple cautiously took his weight off her shoulder.

"How does it look?" she asked cautiously, not wanting to rekindle the previous thread of the conversation.

"Still seeping a bit. Not pumping," he said.

"Good enough," she told him. "Tie the bandage in place and go."

To her immense relief, he didn't argue. He just wrapped more strips from the lab coat around her chest and shoulder, confirmed the address and security information for the rendezvous, and left. Ryder didn't move from her spot on the floor, not wanting to risk starting the bleeding again.

She tried not to worry that he would simply bolt and leave her here after the reminder of what she was guilty of. Of course he wouldn't—he wanted to find Skye, and this was his chance to do so.

Still, though, Ryder was overcome with the feeling that her days of being able to hide from the past were about to come to an end. A deep shudder ran through her... one that had little to do with the onset of shock due to blood loss.

TWELVE

Temple jogged through the streets of the Capital on bare feet, trying not to limp as the blaster burn on his hip and the cuts and bruises on his soles shrieked in protest. He was tired beyond belief, sick of this sense of hovering on the cusp of things either being over, or going completely to shit. A month or more inside the abusive Regime prison system had worn him down, and all he wanted was to find Skye, hug the ever-loving snot out of her, and fall into an actual bed for about a week solid.

Well... that, and he wanted to see Red taken care of so he could shake some answers out of her.

He wasn't quite sure why he couldn't just accept that she was child-murdering Vithii scum and move on. Was it because Skye was apparently involved with her somehow, and he didn't think she would be if Red were truly that kind of person? Or was it because of the heavy weight of old pain that seemed to settle over the woman both times that horrifying charge had been brought up?

Enough. Focus, he ordered himself. The *Vre'Kalsh* building loomed ahead, and inside—hopefully—lay salvation. He slowed to a walk, aware that he'd been attracting odd looks as he hurried along in his stained and rumpled medical scrubs. As a human, attracting attention was never a good thing. He made himself stride purposefully up to the building's side entrance, where he tapped the code into the keypad and did not allow his spine to sag in relief when the lock clicked open.

The lift was out of order. He pressed his lips together in a thin line as he forced his aching body up three flights of stairs. As much as he didn't like the idea of leaving Red on her own in an unlocked restaurant, he had to admit that she wouldn't have been able to make it here with her injury.

Room three-twenty-one was about halfway down the long hallway. Heart pounding with some combination of exertion and anticipation, he pounded on the door. Three short knocks, four long ones, three short ones. He held his breath, wondering if he would see Skye's sweet face when it opened.

He didn't. Instead, he came face to muzzle with a powerful blaster for about the umpteenth time that day, and took a hasty step back. The blaster was held by an imposing Vithii with steel gray eyes and hard features traced with lines of bitterness. The Vithii's gaze raked over him, and one of his eyebrows climbed up his forehead.

"Temple Akenzua?" His voice was a growl, but there was surprise there, too. He glanced behind Temple, as though he expected to see someone else, and his expression narrowed.

"A woman sent me here," Temple said. "Vithii, red hair… said she was working with my sister."

The blaster muzzle dipped, and a grip like iron dragged Temple through the door and shut it behind him.

"Where is she?" the Vithii snapped. "Why isn't she with you?"

He was already moving as he spoke—leaning the blaster rifle against the wall next to the door and sliding into a chair in front of what looked like a cobbled together comm unit.

"She was injured during our escape from the prison. Stabbed in the back. We hid in an evacuated restaurant and I tried to stop the bleeding, then she sent me here for help."

The Vithii rummaged behind the comm unit and came up with a map. "Show me."

Temple blinked exhausted eyes and oriented himself on the map, tracing his finger back from the *Vre'Kalsh* building to the area adjacent to the prison.

"Here," he said, pointing. "I don't know the name of the business, but we got in through an unlocked back entrance in this alley."

The man nodded and gestured imperiously toward a second chair. "Right. Now, sit down before you fall down."

Temple realized that his knees were trembling and took the couple of steps necessary before he could half-fall into the chair. His surroundings went a bit hazy then. He could hear his intimidating host on the comm unit, barking orders, but the individual words slid past his ears without sticking. Only the sense that there was more to do before he could truly relax kept him from keeling over onto the floor and taking a nap as his body was urging him to do.

A rough hand shook his shoulder, rousing him from his dazed state.

"C'mon. There's a hovervan on the way," said the Vithii. "We'll pick up Ryder and meet at a safehouse where we can patch up anyone who needs it, then do the requisite tearful reunions."

This guy didn't seem like the type to have ever had a tearful reunion in his life, but Temple couldn't keep from asking, "And… Skye? Is she okay? Will she be there?"

"Oh, yeah," he said. "She'll be there. I hope you're the open-minded type, though. You've gained a brother-in-law while you were in the slammer."

Temple blinked at him stupidly for a moment before deciding that as long as Skye was all right, she could have married a Vithii mob boss and he didn't really care.

"Okay," he said. "Let's get going."

Even a few minutes of sitting had stiffened his joints and muscles to the point that he was moving like an old man. The three flights of stairs going down were pure torture, but the hovervan was waiting for them as promised, and the upholstered seats felt like heaven. Over the seat back, he met the worried gaze of a dark-eyed human with olive skin and sharp cheekbones.

"I'm Ash," he said, introducing himself with a quick smile that didn't touch the disquiet in his eyes. "You must be Temple. Hang tight for a few more minutes and we'll stage you a long-overdue family homecoming."

It was more than a few minutes. First, they had to get through the perimeter of the evacuated area. Temple saw a generous amount of credits changing hands to make that happen. Then, they backed the van into the alley behind the nameless restaurant. The gray-eyed Vithii ordered Temple to stay where he was, while he and Ash went inside and emerged a couple of minutes later with Red slung between them, her head lolling.

They arranged her on her uninjured side in the back seat, and Temple gave into the impulse to lift her and scoot over a bit so her head was resting on his lap. She seemed pretty far out of it, mumbling nonsense under her breath, and occasionally calling out a name that sounded like *Eldrin*. Not sure what else to do, he removed the scarf she'd tied over her distinctive red hair and used it to blot at the clammy sweat on her forehead.

Eventually, she quieted somewhat, and he started stroking his fingers through her short, spiky hair. When he glanced up, it was to find Ash watching him curiously in the mirror, a look of speculation drifting across his features.

The drive to wherever they were going took even longer. The gray-eyed Vithii was behind the wheel, and they had to wait at several checkpoints as they crept through the city's congested byways. Temple was pretty sure more money had changed hands in the last cycle than he'd earned in the previous year, but eventually both the traffic and the security thinned out.

He didn't recognize this area of the Capital, but it was obviously old. Some of the buildings sliding past the van's windows appeared to be part of the original human colony build, and others were a couple decades newer, but clearly built by people with considerable wealth to spend. The occasional tree or green space began to pop up, unheard of in the central part of the city. Finally, they turned down a narrow street, heading past a few empty parcels where homes had perished to time or fire. At the end of the lane stood an old pile of brick and native stone that looked completely deserted from the outside. The place was grown over in ivy and untamed shrubs. Grass and weeds sprouted from the patchwork of cracks in what had once been the front drive—nature dragging the pavement back into the dry earth.

The van pulled around the side of the giant house and Ash got out, opening a pair of large doors that were slightly bent near the bottom, as if someone had carelessly backed into them at one point and never fixed them. The vehicle eased through the gap into a generous garage area, out of sight from prying eyes.

Temple felt himself finally starting to relax, as the reality of being far away from the prison in an untraceable location gradually filtered past the stress and shock. He looked down at the woman whose head still rested on his thigh. She had settled into sleep or unconsciousness, no longer twisting restlessly.

The side door slid open and Ash peered in, flashing him another unconvincing smile. "End of the line," he said, his Old Earth British accent seeming more pronounced with worry as he looked down at Red's still body.

A moment later, a huge, hulking form appeared behind the slender human and moved him aside with a hand on each of his shoulders.

"She's alive, Pax," Ash said quickly, as the figure leaned through the van door—the gap barely wide enough for his broad frame.

A jolt of instinctive, animal reaction made Temple's heart jump behind his ribcage as he saw the filigree of shining implants covering half of the Vithii's face.

"*What the fuck!*" he snarled, instinct propelling him to lean forward, shielding Red's body from the vision of death looming over them.

Cyborg.

The most feared creation on Ilarius… devised by the same twisted military minds that had conceived of a bioweapon aimed at humans.

"Whoa! Easy, there," Ash interjected, as Temple cast around the enclosed space for anything that might make a weapon against a creature that could pick him up and snap his body in two like a twig. "Pax—reassure *Skye's brother* that you're not here to bash heads, will you? Sorry, Temple, neither of us thought to warn you…"

The cyborg's flat gaze flickered up to Temple's for a moment, and he shivered.

"I am not here to bash heads," the creature said in a voice with a faint mechanical edge. "Now, move, before I change my mind."

"Not helpful, big man," Ash muttered, running a hand through his shoulder-length black hair. "Look, Ryder's our medic. But Pax has experience in battlefield medicine, and I promise you he's not at all like what you're thinking. He's best equipped to treat her wound, and I don't like how pale she's looking. Will you please trust us, so we can get her inside and help her?"

Temple's heart was still surging under the fresh burst of adrenaline. Could he trust them? What the hell choice did he have? Cautiously, he straightened away from his protective crouch over Red's body, never taking his eyes off the dangerous figure in front of him.

The cyborg didn't speak; only reached in and scooped Red up with effortless strength, lifting her out of the van and cradling her in arms that looked like tree trunks. Temple followed, moving carefully, every joint in his body protesting the last few days as he climbed out ungracefully and braced himself on unsteady legs.

The cyborg—*Pax*?—held Red as though she were made of glass, an indecipherable expression on his face as he looked down at her resting in his arms. The strangest sensation crept over Temple as he watched the unlikely scene. It felt like jealousy... and that was *completely mental*. Worry? Sure. Stark terror? Too fucking right. But why in the hell would he possibly feel the urge to stomp over and get in the face of a *gods-damned Vithii cyborg* so he could drag the prickly Vithii woman he was holding out of his steel-reinforced grip?

Temple realized that he was in real danger of finally losing his shit after a day spent alternating between anger, terror, and the expectation of imminent death.

"I... think I need to sit down," he said faintly.

Ash's hand closed around his upper arm, steadying him, and there was sympathy in his voice when he said, "I don't doubt it. Come on, let's—"

The words were cut off by the growl of an approaching engine. *Hoverbike*, Temple identified, as the Vithii guy who'd been driving the van moved to swing open one of the garage doors. The bike pulled in, two figures straddling it. The one on the back swung off almost before it came to a complete stop, revealing a slender female figure.

Temple caught his breath sharply, recognizing that gawky human frame. "*Skye*," he breathed hoarsely. "Oh, my gods..."

Skye tore the black helmet from her head and let it drop. With a wordless cry, she launched herself at him. Ash released his grip just in time for Temple to catch his foster sister in his arms, staggering back a step as their arms tangled around each other and *squeezed*.

"Temple," Skye sobbed against his neck. "*Temple*—oh, prophets! You're here, you're all right..."

Temple felt himself tearing up as well, and hid his face in her tangled blonde hair. "I can't leave you alone for a minute without you getting into trouble, can I, pipsqueak?" he whispered, and squeezed his eyes shut as choked laughter tangled together with her sobs.

"You're one to talk," she managed after a moment, pulling away enough that she could frame his face in her hands. She swallowed hard, salt water still streaming down her cheeks. "Temple... I'm so sorry. Dad's dead. They shot him as we were trying to escape. I... couldn't save him..."

He pulled her back against his chest. "I know, Skye. There's nothing you could have done, sis. But you did it! You got the antidote out. You saved the humans in the Capital."

She gave him a final hard squeeze and straightened again. "It wasn't me. I couldn't have done a damned thing on my own." She gestured around with a movement of her head. "It was the others. They saved us. They saved both of us." She took a shuddering breath, obviously trying to drag her composure back together. "Temple, there's someone I want you to meet. My bondmate—Hunter Tarthasian."

Temple looked up and realized that another person had approached and was standing behind Skye, wearing black hoverbike leathers and holding his helmet under his left arm. Temple's first confused impression was of an imposing Vithii with pale green eyes that cut like lasers.

"Temple," the man said in a resonant voice with iron at its core, "I am more pleased than I can say to see you reunited with your sister. Your absence has rested heavily on her heart these past weeks." Before Temple could draw breath to react to the distinctive raven-feather tattoos emerging from the Vithii's collar and running up his neck, the Rook—the fucking *Rook*—continued in a voice of command, "Ash. What is Ryder's condition?"

"Pax took her inside," Ash replied promptly. "She was unconscious, but her vitals seemed strong."

The Vithii nodded. "Has everyone else returned safely?"

"All accounted for," said the gray-eyed Vithii who'd driven them.

"Skye," Temple said slowly, staring at the face he knew from a hundred vidcasts. The face of one of the most notorious criminals in the Seven Systems. "That's… he's…"

"Yeah," Skye said on a sigh, stretching up and pulling him down enough to press a kiss to his forehead. "He is. Come inside. There are a lot of things I need to catch you up on."

Temple let himself be led inside. He insisted on first seeing where the cyborg had taken Red, just to reassure himself that she really was being cared for. The makeshift infirmary was nothing fancy, but it was clean and well lit, and Red lay facedown on a medical cot, her chest rising and falling in a regular rhythm. The massive hybrid soldier peered down at her shoulder, the wound illuminated by the white light coming from an implant at his temple.

He glanced up at the intrusion. "Since you're ambulatory, your injuries will have to wait until I'm finished here," he told Temple in that flat, raspy voice.

Temple nodded, reassured that she truly would get the treatment she needed. "I'm only here to check on her," he replied.

The cyborg flickered an eyebrow and returned to his patient without another word. Skye's hand squeezed his shoulder and urged him away from the door.

"Pax will take care of her," his foster sister said quietly. "We should get out of his way and leave him to it."

Half a cycle later, Temple was installed on a dusty sofa in a generously sized sitting room, his mind whirling with everything Skye had just told him. He'd been surprised as hell when Jonah, of all people, had wandered in to join them with another Vithii—this one a copper-haired and golden-eyed man who looked like he could bench-press Temple one-handed without breaking a sweat.

Jonah looked about as shell-shocked as Temple felt, but at least he was safe and out of that hellhole of a prison.

Temple took a breath and tried to recap what he'd just been told over the course of the last few minutes. "So, let me get this straight, Skye. The Rook and his notorious criminal gang are actually the good guys, he helped you get the antidote to the Premiere's bioweapon into the water system, and now you're married to him. Vithii-style."

"Pretty much," Skye confirmed.

She was sitting next to him, gripping his hand like she was afraid he'd disappear into the ether if she didn't hold him in place. Temple understood the impulse—he was gripping her right back. The Rook—whose name was apparently Hunter—was seated in a chair across from them, watching Skye with indulgent affection. Temple had to admit, it was pretty fucking hard to reconcile that look of obvious love with the monster the news vids made him out to be.

His green gaze moved to Temple. "We've been unable to locate your foster mother, I'm sorry to say."

Temple nodded. "I tried to ask around when I was in the prison, and couldn't find any indication she was being held there."

"Ryder was able to confirm that she was not a current or former inmate at the prison. She had access to the prisoner records before she was compromised," Hunter said.

Ash was curled up in another chair, his chin resting on one raised knee. "We'll keep searching. Even with her husband dead, Stella Chantrell still has strategic value as long as Skye is free. It's unlikely they'll execute her if they think she may be useful."

Skye flinched next to him at the mention of their father's death, and he pressed his shoulder against her in support.

"You're right," he agreed. "Thank you for doing this. *All* of this."

Ash gave him a quicksilver smile. "It's what we're here for."

Jonah had been quiet, picking at the hem of the borrowed tunic someone had managed to scare up for him. Now, he looked up at the others. "So, what's next?"

"Next?" Hunter echoed. "Next, we let Ryder have a chance to recover, and find someplace more secure to hunker down for a bit while we plan our next move."

As if the words had given Temple's body permission to finally stop fighting, he sagged against the back of the couch. His burned hip and abused feet throbbed, demanding attention, but even with the discomfort he thought he could probably sleep for a week.

"Okay," he said. "Yeah. I think that's a plan I can get behind."

THIRTEEN

Ryder blinked awake, disoriented in the low light. She was lying on her left side on a soft surface. Her mouth felt like a small animal had crawled into it and died of some kind of slow wasting disease. Unfortunately, in her rather extensive experience, waking up groggy and not knowing where you were was generally a bad sign.

She tried to roll upright, only to collapse back on the cot when her right arm wouldn't hold her weight. The back of her right shoulder ached and pulled, bringing with it the memory of sudden agony as a blade slid into her from behind. The prison—

"Ryder!" The familiar cadence of Ash's voice cut into her thoughts, dragging them away from memories of unwashed bodies and the din of weapons fire. "Easy now—you're safe…"

"Do not attempt to rise," came Pax's metallic rasp. "The repairs to your shoulder are still at a delicate stage."

The breath left her lungs in a rush and she sagged back against the mattress in relief.

"Where—?" she croaked, the word barely audible as it emerged past her cracked lips.

"Location Seven," Pax replied promptly. Anticipating her next question, he added, "You were successful in retrieving Skye's foster brother. He had some injuries, but nothing terribly serious. I patched him up once I was done with you."

"Lights, twenty-five percent," Ash said, and Ryder squinted a bit as the levels rose to reveal the pair of them hovering on either side of her cot.

Ash retrieved a bottle with a straw from a table nearby. "Drink. It's just water and electrolytes... Pax wanted to see how you were feeling before trying anything more substantial."

She let him support her head so she could take a few sips of the liquid. It slipped down her dry throat, cool and soothing. When she was done, he eased her back down to lie flat. She cleared her throat experimentally before speaking.

"I want a word with whoever came up with this rescue plan," she said. "It was complete shit."

"Everyone's a critic," Ash said. "You were supposed to duck when the guy with the knife came at you."

"He came at me *from behind*," she pointed out. "And that wasn't even the aspect I was complaining about."

"I can't think of everything," Ash defended, "but I'm sorry someone put a hole in your shoulder. I do feel quite bad about that part."

"How serious is it?" she asked Pax. In addition to the weakness in her arm, her right hand still felt numb and tingly.

"The blade penetrated the trapezius muscle and partway through the rhomboid," he said. "It avoided any major veins or arteries, but there was some nerve irritation. Nothing appeared severed. I chose to use standard tissue regeneration tech and wait for you to regain consciousness so you could decide for yourself if you wanted to use bots. You also had a cracked rib, but it's healing well after the standard bone-knitting treatment."

She nodded. "Thank you. Did you record any footage of the stab injury I could look at?"

"Yes. I'll download it to a terminal for you to review."

She carefully moved her fingers, relieved that her dexterity seemed unaffected. Blood tingled as she stretched her hand and wrist, as though circulation were returning. It could have been worse.

"I'm sure you'll be playing the piano again in no time, Doc," Ash said.

She shot him a look. "I'm not a doctor, Ash, and I don't play the piano." She refocused, trying to get her scattered brain back in the game. "Pax? You said Temple was injured as well?"

"Scrapes and abrasions from running on bare feet, along with a bruised jaw, minor concussion, and a blaster graze on his left hip. The burns were mostly second-degree, with a very small area of third-degree damage at the center."

"He also has a thing for you, Doc," Ash added helpfully, "in case it escaped your attention during all the excitement."

Ryder stared at him as if he'd grown a second head. "I beg your pardon?"

"Look, I'm just throwing it out there," Ash said. "Do with the information as you wish."

Her eyes narrowed.

"No need for the death glare. If it makes you feel better, forget I said anything," he said, lifting his hands in a mock fending-off gesture, before turning his attention to Pax. "So, are you done with your patient for the moment, big guy? If so, I need a private word with her."

"Yes. For now," Pax said. "Don't wear her out."

Pax left, closing the door behind him with a soft *click*. Ryder continued to pin Ash with a glare, but it was gaining a suspicious edge now. Their resident human tended not to have much in the way of a verbal filter at the best of times, which made her wonder what he would consider sensitive enough to warrant a private conversation.

"What?" she asked, her growing wariness emerging as curtness.

Ash sighed and dragged a chair around to sit next to the cot, dropping forward until his elbows rested on his knees, his fingers tangled together loosely in front of him. He regarded her with a faint frown on his face, and worry clouding his dark eyes.

"Ash, *what*?" she asked again, more sharply this time. Not liking the feeling of creeping vulnerability that came from lying here like an invalid while Ash looked at her with that unhappy expression.

"When you missed the check-in, we knew we had very little time to act, Ryder," he said. "I needed every bit of information I could lay hands on, and I had no way of determining what might be useful and what wouldn't. I... searched for any records on you that I could find. Records under your real name."

The bottom dropped out of Ryder's stomach.

"How—?" she began, only to cut herself off, and whisper, "*Pax*."

"Yes," Ash confirmed quietly. "But, Ryder— please don't blame him. He only wanted you back safe. That's all any of us wanted."

"You shouldn't have looked," Ryder rasped.

"I'm sorry," Ash said. "Does Pax know? About... the reason you lost your medical license?"

Her heart was pounding. It was probably a good thing no one had bothered to hook her up to a pulse monitor.

"Yes," she said, barely audible.

Ash nodded slowly, his eyes not moving from her face. "All right. I just… thought you should know. I *am* sorry, Ryder."

"Get out," she managed.

Ash's dark eyebrows twitched, the furrow before them deepening before his expression smoothed into a mask that showed nothing. "Okay. Pax will be back in a little while. Try to get some rest, eh?"

She looked away, not answering, staring at the cracked plaster of the ceiling rather than at him. She heard his soft sigh, followed by the chair scraping back and the sound of his footsteps. The door opened and closed softly, leaving her alone.

Aryderlyn Erisuel. The monster who'd experimented on an innocent child. The untouchable *grei'kaapt*.

A horribly tight choking sensation wrapped around her chest and throat. She swallowed hard several times until she could breath again. The implication of Ash's innocent snooping buzzed around her thoughts like circling insects.

Pax knew—some of it, at least. But Pax was a cyborg. In his eyes, the usefulness her medical and scientific knowledge brought to the group outweighed any potential threat she might pose. He wasn't concerned with anything as ephemeral as morality. That was the purview of the meatbags; cyborgs dealt in practicalities.

The same thing could not be said of the others, however. Hunter was one of the most morally upright people Ryder had ever met. And while Kade and Draven might scoff at the concept of nobility, they followed a strict code of conduct nonetheless. Skye came from a normal, human civilian background that made her both principled and somewhat naive about the realities of the world—though that naïveté had admittedly taken something of a beating, of late.

No doubt Skye's foster brother Temple was the same, for all that he'd waved it off when Ryder had tried to warn him what sort of person she was. They'd been in the middle of a crisis, where Ryder was Temple's ticket out of prison and back to Skye. Of course he'd been willing to temporarily overlook her sins. He'd needed her at the time.

Of all of them, Ash was probably the most morally… flexible. It made sense that he wouldn't understand the true import of what he'd found buried in her past—and what he had no doubt already reported to the others. She tried to tell herself that his intentions had been good. Even though it had been a shitty rescue plan, it was still the reason she and Temple were alive and free.

That nobility Ryder had noted earlier would probably stay Hunter's hand until Ryder recovered from her injuries, but after that, she had no doubt that he'd cut her loose whether Pax argued against it or not. If she'd still had two functioning neurons to bang together, she'd be relieved by that fact. What the Shadow Wing was doing was suicidally dangerous, as evidenced by the last few days.

So why did the idea of leaving make her body go cold?

She could probably go underground again as a back-alley sawbones, as she had done after she'd fled Jodor's first attempt to have her killed. Working for the gangs, providing no-questions-asked medical care for criminals who wouldn't dare show their faces in a real hospital. A hazardous profession, but practically a frolic in the park compared to what she was doing now.

She had options, she told herself, trying to beat down the feelings of panic. She would wait things out, see how the others reacted, and go from there.

When Pax returned, she asked him for the footage of her shoulder, knowing that regaining full use and feeling in her hand was more important than ever if she was about to lose her paltry handful of allies and her only source of backup. To her relief, the damage was nothing that wouldn't heal, thanks to the cyborg's deft handling of the tissue regeneration process. She would be left with a scar that ached when the weather changed, but it was hardly her first.

Reassured, she requested some nutrient broth and a sedative to help her sleep. Pax gave her a lingering look before agreeing, and she briefly wondered what thoughts were hidden away behind his impassive face. A few minutes later, her worries faded away beneath the blank nothingness of exhausted sleep.

◆

Low voices roused her from her old, recurring dream of a child crying, bewilderment and pain behind the plaintive sobs as Ryder pressed her hand to the cold glass of a quarantine unit. She gasped and scrambled upright, her shoulder protesting the sudden movement.

"Whoa!" came a female voice, human and startled. "Ryder, hey—take it easy, there. I think you were having a nightmare."

Ryder's heart was racing so fast it made her feel dizzy, and she gulped in deep breaths as she tried to get her bearings. Location Seven. The prison escape. A stab wound, healing now. Ash, accidentally bringing her whole world crashing down around her shoulders.

"Hey, Red," said a second voice. "Talk to me. You okay, there? I haven't had a chance to thank you since the restaurant."

Temple.

"What are you doing here?" she asked, addressing the question to both of them.

It was Skye who answered. "Like Temple said, we were worried about you. We came in to sit with you for a bit, that's all."

"Oh," Ryder said, somewhat stupidly.

For some reason, she was having difficulty getting their words to match up with her brain. Why would they want to sit with her? She supposed that Skye's gratitude for getting Temple back... might conceivably override her disgust over what Ash had found? Or maybe she felt guilty for Ryder having been captured while searching for her brother? But, even if that were the case, surely Pax would have told them already that she was stable and recovering.

"How are you feeling?" Skye asked, thankfully letting go of the part about the nightmare. "Pax said you'd be okay in a few days."

She tried to calm her thundering pulse, hating the way her body was betraying her, making her feel weak and off-balance. She'd spent years cultivating a hard-as-nails persona; she no longer knew how to relate to the world without it.

"I'm fine," she said, "no thanks to Ash and whoever else came up with the hare-brained idea of using a prison riot as a rescue plan."

Skye looked uncomfortable, which suited Ryder perfectly at the moment. Let someone else be on the back foot for a bit.

"I'm sorry you were there in the first place," she said. "I didn't mean for any of this to happen."

Ryder started to snap, *'Not as sorry as I am,'* but her eyes wandered to Temple's concerned face, and the words died on her lips.

"It could have been worse," she said instead… which was technically true, she supposed. Her eyes traveled critically over Temple's body. He looked tired—his posture slumping a bit and a hint of grayness lurking under his dark complexion. "How are your injuries faring? Did Pax take care of you? He doesn't have a lot of experience treating humans."

Temple waved the question off. "Just tired. There may be some scarring on my hip, but who the hell cares? And I had to do the concussion protocol bullshit last night, which cut into my sleep."

"Yes," Skye said, affection lacing her voice. "Heaven forbid you should miss out on your beauty rest for a tiny little thing like potential brain damage. Not that anyone would be able to tell the difference, Mister *'I'll act as the decoy and get my ass thrown into prison.'*"

At least something good had come of all this, Ryder thought. Seeing the two humans together went some way toward balancing out the darkness licking at the edges of her life.

"Speaking of rest," she said, forcing her voice into its usual acerbic tone.

Skye blushed. "Sorry, Ryder. We'll get out of your hair now. I'm glad you're recovering. And… thank you."

Ryder made a vague gesture with her left hand. She was really starting to wonder if anyone had bothered to tell Skye about her unsavory past yet. Maybe Hunter and the others hadn't wanted to upset her when she was obviously so happy to have her brother back safely?

"I'll be along in a minute," Temple told his sister, flashing her a quick, affectionate smile and not budging from his seat near the bed. Skye smiled back and squeezed his shoulder, giving Ryder a final glance of gratitude as she left the room.

When she was gone, Temple turned his full attention to Ryder, studying her for several long seconds. Feeling unaccountably self-conscious, Ryder scowled at him.

"You have something to say?" she asked, wondering if he'd stayed behind to tell her some variation of 'hey, thanks so much for getting me out of prison, but since you're a child-murderer, don't expect me to interact with you after this.'

He shrugged. "Pretty much the same thing Skye had to say. I'm glad you're recovering, and thank you for risking your life for me," he said. There was a pause as she waited for the rest, and he did not disappoint her. "Well, and also this…"

With that, he rose from the chair and bent over her. She sat frozen in shock as he leaned closer, until his lips brushed hers in what her dazed mind identified as a human kiss.

It was… odd, and soft, and intimate, and Ryder had absolutely no clue what to do with it. Temple's callused fingers brushed the side of her face as she sat motionless, trying to wrap her brain around what was happening. When he pulled away, her lips were tingling and her cheek felt warm where his fingers had touched it.

"What… are you doing?" she managed after a couple of seconds of her mouth opening and closing with nothing coming out.

He huffed a breath and rubbed the back of his neck with one hand. "It's called *a kiss,*" he joked. "It's a human thing. You might have seen it before on a holodrama once or twice over the course of your lifetime…?"

She stared at him. "But… why?"

He stared right back. "Because you're beautiful, and brilliant, and you risked your life to save me when you didn't even know me. Because I realized yesterday that I'm starting to have feelings for you… and because I wanted to."

"Temple," she said, "that's insane. I told you what I was; what I'd done."

He continued to look at her as though she were a puzzle he wanted to unlock.

"About the charges?" he said. "Yes. You did. And I told you I didn't believe you."

She tried to find words. "Whether you choose to believe it or not, it's true."

He lifted an eyebrow, tilting his head as he examined her. "No. It's not. You can say that all day long, but your eyes tell a different story. If you ever decide you want to share that story with me, you know where to find me."

With that, he turned and left the room, throwing a glance over his shoulder at her before following in his sister's footsteps.

FOURTEEN

The following day, sat listlessly at the scuffed wooden table in the house's massive kitchen area, poking at his food while Skye and Ash chatted sporadically about the news reports filtering in from the rest of the city. While the meal wasn't exactly home cooking, it wasn't bad, either—certainly not when compared to the bacteria-laden slop that comprised inmate nutrition at the prison.

Skye paused, watching him. "Eat," she said. "You've lost a ton of weight in the last month." She tilted her head, birdlike. "What's wrong? You're moping."

He smiled at her with affection. "And you're nagging, pipsqueak," he pointed out without rancor.

"Maybe so," she admitted, "but, seriously, you need to eat. What's up?"

"I realize it's not exactly *haute cuisine*," Ash offered. "But if this doesn't appeal, there are several different varieties of Redi-Meals in the pantry."

Temple shook his head. "No, it's not that. Please, don't mind me. I'm just distracted, and not sleeping so great."

Ash regarded him for a few moments. "Hmm. Thoughts of our red-haired Vithii doctor keeping you up at night, perhaps?"

Temple was quickly growing to appreciate Ash for both his quick mind and his dry British humor.

There were times, though, when both of those qualities hit a bit too close to home for comfort.

"She's not a doctor," he said absently.

Ash raised an eyebrow. "Thoughts of our red-haired *former* doctor, then?"

Now, Skye was giving him a curious look as well. "Something you want to tell me, big brother?"

Temple frowned and put down his fork, rubbing the bridge of his nose between his thumb and forefinger. "What do you know about her, Skye?" he asked in lieu of an answer.

Skye seemed to give the question serious consideration before she replied. "Let's see. Prickly as an *indirian* cactus, doesn't suffer fools gladly, one of the most brilliant people I've ever met. Gets weird whenever you bring up her medical degree. Scary as shit?"

Temple couldn't help the laugh that shook free of his chest, and he thought he heard Ash give a quiet snort as well.

"I figured out most of that already, thanks," he said. "I was hoping for a bit more detail to fill in the blanks."

Skye shrugged. "Ash knows her better than I do."

"I've known her *longer* than you have," Ash corrected, "which is not necessarily the same thing as knowing her *better*."

For someone who seemed so open, Ash could be a surprisingly hard one to read. Still, Temple was getting a vibe from him like he was holding back, or perhaps hoping that Temple would move on to a different subject.

"It isn't *necessarily* the same," Temple shot back, "but it *might* be the same. So, any additional insights into why she's locked down so tight? Because for someone who's brilliant, beautiful, courageous, and scary as shit, she sure doesn't seem to think much of herself."

Skye's eyes grew wide. "Oh, my gods. Ash is right—you do have a thing for her!" She turned pleading eyes on Ash. "Come on, Ash, throw him a bone, *please*? You've *got* to want to see this go down at least as much as I do."

Ash smiled, a bit wistfully if Temple was any judge.

"Oh, believe me—I most certainly do," he said, then sobered. "What else can I tell you? Ryder is a good person with a difficult past. A past, I hasten to add, that's not my story to tell. But I do hope that you'll ask her to tell you that story herself."

Temple deflated a bit. "I already did. It seems to be a highly effective way to get her to shut down completely."

"Then I hope you'll ask her again," Ash said. "Because something about that story is eating her away from the inside out, and I have reason to believe that it's only going to get worse as time goes on." His eyes grew far away. "There's only so long you can bottle up your pain and regret... before pain and regret are all that you have left."

<hr>

In Ryder's dream, Jodor was looming over her, anger and desperation clouding his mud-brown eyes. "You're a doctor, aren't you?" he asked. "So *fix this*. I don't care what you have to do. It must have been your genetics at fault in the first place. It certainly wasn't mine. You either make him better, Lyn, or you pack your things and go!"

Jodor spun before she could even draw breath to answer, not that she could seem to get air into her lungs with the tight, invisible band strapped around her chest. The printouts of medical and genetic reports fluttered around her where he'd tossed them away in disgust as he stormed out, settling slowly onto the floor like wounded Ilarian flutter-wings.

The terrible, sick certainty that there was nothing she could possibly do in the short amount of time she had left was like hot lead balling inside her gut. No drug or procedure could alter a Vithii's genetic code throughout the entire body—

She gasped in a breath, as an idea both horrible and wonderful assailed her between one pounding heartbeat and the next.

No drug or procedure.

Holy prophets.

Holy prophets!

But… could she get access to the technology in time? She would never be able to do it through regular channels. There was no way the medical board would okay something so experimental without months or years of laboratory and clinical trials.

Eldrin didn't have years. He had weeks.

Suddenly needing to see him… *needing* to confirm with her own eyes that he was still alive, still here, that he hadn't slipped away, she jogged out of the conference room and down the echoing hallways to the quarantine wing. The nurse at the check-in station looked at her like she'd gone mad and opened her mouth as if to say something, but she was already gone. The glass wall of the quarantine unit glinted under the harsh overhead lighting, and Ryder slid to a stop, pressing her hands to it.

Inside, Eldrin was sleeping restlessly, his too-thin chest rising and falling under the bandages. Her panic started to ebb—he was still here, it wasn't too late. She flattened her palms against the cool barrier, spreading her fingers.

"I have an idea, baby," she said, knowing he couldn't hear her and wouldn't understand even if he could. "Hang on for me. I think I know how to save you."

⁕

Ryder jerked awake with a gasp. She was alone in the medical room, evidently considered far enough along in her recovery not to rate a babysitter any longer. The ache of old pain she felt had nothing to do with her shoulder and everything to do with her heart. Tired of feeling like she was lying around waiting for the metaphorical axe to fall, she cautiously rolled into a sitting position and put her bare feet on the floor.

She noted that while someone—probably Pax—had gotten an oversized shirt onto her after her shoulder and rib had been treated, no one had wanted to deal with her below the waist if it wasn't medically necessary. Not even a cyborg. She was still wearing the much-abused scrub bottoms, stiff in the back with the dried blood that had dripped down from the stab wound.

At least someone had left a clean pair of underwear and polysynth unisex trousers draped over a nearby chair back. *Underwear.* Now there was something you didn't appreciate nearly enough until you'd gone a few days without it.

She glanced around. After a while, the safehouses all started to blur together. Trying to remember the layout of this place, she grabbed the clothing and made her unsteady way out into the hall. The lav was just about as dire as she remembered it being, but it had a showerhead and when you turned it on, water came out… albeit not with very much pressure and not really spraying in the direction you might expect it to.

And not, apparently, in any temperature other than cold.

Still, someone had acquired soap, so it was marginally better than living in a cave. She stepped in and washed herself quickly, hindered by the limited range of motion in her right arm. She could feel that it was improving rapidly as the regeneration therapy did its work, but the muscles that had been torn and damaged would still need strengthening.

Another thing to worry about, on her ever-growing list of things to worry about.

She stepped out a few moments later, shivering, and toweled herself off before dressing. Deciding there was no point in skulking around like a criminal—and wasn't *that* just the most ironic thing ever—she headed for the central living area. A glance out one of the tall, narrow windows showed that it was late afternoon. She'd slept much of the day away, even without a sedative. She supposed she must have needed it.

This place was set up with four wings surrounding a central atrium. It was the same house they'd sheltered in after Hunter had been injured in the fight at the water treatment plant—the one where he and Skye had their bonding ceremony.

As she approached the less damaged of the two symmetrically arranged living rooms—the one in the east wing—she heard the low sound of voices and knew that she'd guessed right. Steeling herself and with no idea what reception she was likely to get, Ryder walked into the room with a sure stride and her head held high.

Hunter, Kade, Pax, and Draven were seated in a loose semicircle around the low table surrounded by chairs and couches, evidently holding a war council of sorts. Draven, facing the doorway, reacted first. He rose from his seat, his heavy features lighting up in evident pleasure, throwing her off balance.

"Ryder! You're up. Come in, come in—we were just discussing our next move," he said, making a move toward her as though to help her across the room. She frowned and waved him off.

"Welcome back," Kade said dryly. "Now, help me convince Pax that we need to get out of the Capital for a while, until things cool down."

"Sit down, Ryder," Hunter added. "How are you feeling?"

Like I'm going mad, she thought, but she only said, "Fine."

"How is your range of motion in the shoulder?" Pax asked.

"About like you'd expect," she said, knowing she sounded churlish. "Don't fuss."

"I will design a regimen of physical therapy exercises, now that you are recovering your strength," he said, ignoring her bad temper as he always did.

The only possible explanation was that Ash hadn't told the others… or hadn't told the others *yet*. Again, that sense of waiting for a heavy blade to swing down and slice her life to pieces overcame her. The idea of sitting here discussing her recovery with these men who would abhor her if they knew what she'd been accused of—what she'd *done*—was almost sickening.

Hunter was addressing her again, and she blinked, trying to bridge the gap between the world inside her head, where everything was falling apart, and the world outside of it, where it wasn't. *Yet.*

"I regret that I wasn't able to identify you when you emerged from the prison," he was saying. "I was the one watching the main prisoner entrance, but somehow I missed you in the confusion. Had I not, you wouldn't have been forced to wait alone for help until Ash and Kade got there."

Ryder shook her head. "Not your fault. I covered my head so my red hair would be less recognizable." She took a steadying breath. "My bondmate was there, at the prison. He wants me dead. I thought he might have had the guards looking out for me specifically. Figured there was no point in making it easy for them."

The men were silent for a moment, obviously not sure what to do with that piece of information. Which was fair, since she wasn't sure why she'd told them, either.

Pax was the first to find his tongue. "I withdraw my previous reservations. Kade is correct—we should get out of the city."

Kade raised his eyebrows and threw her a look. "Oh. Well, that was easy. Too bad you didn't show up fifteen minutes ago, Ryder."

"I have no problem with that," Hunter said. "I doubt Ash will go for it, though."

Ryder found herself thinking, *if Ash isn't with us, maybe he'll be less likely to tell the others what he learned*, and immediately felt a fresh rush of self-loathing. Prophets, what kind of a pathetic worm was she becoming?

Kade grunted. "Ash is determined to follow the course he's on even if it kills him. The worst part is, he usually ends up getting intel we couldn't have gotten any other way. Given that any one of us could end up getting vaped at pretty much any moment, maybe he's not wrong."

Predictably, Draven's face darkened like storm clouds obscuring the sun. "Nothing could make what he's doing worthwhile."

Hunter shot him a quelling look. "Ash makes his own choices, Draven."

"Yeah," Draven shot back. "He does. *Stupid* ones."

"Is he still here?" Ryder asked, knowing that Ash's… situation… made it difficult for him to be absent from his usual haunts for any extended length of time.

"He went back to the central district to take care of some things," Hunter said, "but he plans to return. He arranged for it to look like he'd contracted an illness when you failed to check in and he needed to help us stage the riot."

"Forged hospital records and everything, apparently," Kade said. "I might have to fight the urge to thump him whenever I'm forced to spend more than an hour at a time with him, but even I have to admit that he's thorough. Honestly, I still can't believe he reprogrammed an airlock maintenance program into a security system virus in less than thirty-six hours."

"I still can't believe that it *worked*," Draven muttered.

"And I still can't believe you all thought inciting a prison riot was in any way a rational rescue plan," Ryder grumbled, unable to help herself.

"Never disparage a successful strategy," Pax said, unruffled as always.

A sudden wave of tiredness washed over her, and she scrubbed at her face with her hand. How easy it was to fall into the normal give and take with these four. How easy to forget that it could all come crashing down at any moment.

"You still look like shit, Ryder," Kade said, not unkindly. "Go back to bed."

"All is well, for the moment," Hunter told her. "If anything important happens, I'll make sure you're informed."

Giving up, Ryder nodded and moved to leave, pausing at the door. "All right. I'm done playing invalid, though," she said. "If anyone needs me I'll be in the bedroom I used last time we were here. At least the mattress in there is more comfortable."

FIFTEEN

Unfortunately, a comfortable mattress did nothing to stop Ryder's nightmares. Which was why, in the wee hours of the morning, she was sitting on the stone bench in the atrium of the old house, letting the faint stirring of the breeze carry the distant tang of the ocean to her nostrils.

The ache in her shoulder had transformed into a deep, intense itching sensation. After her mind had once again jolted her awake with the plaintive sound of a crying toddler, her shoulder ensured that she would not be getting back to sleep anytime soon. She just… wanted all this to *stop*.

For a few years, she had reached the point where her past didn't dominate every blasted moment of the present. Now, it was clear that had been a temporary respite, not a steppingstone toward better things to come. Jodor was still alive. She was a child murderer. Jodor would stop at nothing until she was dead, and he was free of the stain of their bond. If she wasn't careful, the people around her would get caught in the crossfire, and their blood would also be on her hands.

Maybe the best thing she could do for any of them would be to leave. Hadn't she been resigned to leaving anyway? At least if she did, she wouldn't have to wonder about when that metaphorical axe would fall on her head.

A soft noise in the atrium startled her from her dark musings. She whirled, cursing under her breath as her shoulder protested.

"Hey," Temple said. "Sorry, didn't mean to startle you. I didn't realize you'd be out here. Can't sleep?"

Temple wandered up and plopped down beside her on the bench, his arm brushing hers as he braced his hands on the rough stone of the seat.

"Something like that," Ryder said cautiously.

"Yeah, me neither. I think a month spent languishing in that damned pit of a prison permanently screwed up my diurnal clock." He arched his neck to one side and then the other, vertebrae popping. "Also, my dreams... aren't the best right now. I thought I'd come out here and at least get some fresh air. I still can't quite get over this place. It's amazing."

He looked up at the rustling branches of the old *chik'taap* tree that protected the atrium from aerial or satellite surveillance, and breathed in deeply.

Ryder snorted. "Sure... if you don't mind the moldy walls, crumbling plaster, and lack of hot water, it's great."

He glanced over at her, the glow of filtered moonlight illuminating his raised eyebrow. "Red, I'm disappointed in you. I mean, *look* at this house. Have you no sense of history?"

"Absolutely none," she agreed, falling into the relaxed conversation utterly despite herself.

He huffed out a soft breath.

"So," he continued, "I told you what's keeping me up at night. What's keeping you up at night?"

"The past," she whispered, without thinking.

Rather than jump on the statement, Temple let it escape into the night air, wafting its way into the tree branches above them like smoke. They were silent for several minutes, each thinking their own thoughts.

Eventually, Temple drew breath to speak again. "Who's Eldrin, Ryder?" he asked softly.

Ryder's breath locked in her chest, and she nearly choked.

"*Where did you hear that name*?" she demanded harshly.

Temple continued to look at her, curious and without judgment. "You were mumbling it in the back of the van, when you were delirious." He paused, as though debating whether to continue. "That's the name of the child who died, isn't it?" he asked eventually.

Ice cascaded through Ryder's veins, the past crashing through the barrier of time, threatening to crush her. *No*, she thought. *No, no, I can't do this. I can't do this any more. Please, prophets, please— just make it all stop.*

Without a word, she scrambled gracelessly to her feet and fled back into the house.

✦

Shit, shit, shit. Temple silently cursed himself as he followed Ryder into the depths of the sprawling structure and watched her disappear into one of the many bedrooms, the door closing firmly behind her. He could just make out the sound of the lock clicking a moment later.

He stood frozen for several moments, trying to decide what to do next. He decided after running through several possible scenarios that the logical course of action was to go curse out the British wanker who'd goaded him into confronting Red again, when she'd already basically told him to fuck off once. This had been Ash's idea; Ash could damned well help him deal with the fallout.

He turned left down the corridor and counted doors from the end of the hall in the south wing, not wanting to accidentally barge in on Kade or, gods forbid, Hunter and Skye. Pax was probably keeping watch somewhere, but whereas Ash deserved to be dragged into this, Temple thought Pax might just rip his head from his spine if he told him what had happened. To say that the cyborg seemed a little bit protective of Ryder was like saying that the Premiere was a little bit racist.

Once he was certain he had the right room, Temple quietly eased the door open. "Ash?" he hissed. The lights were low—five percent, maybe—but not turned off completely. As his eyes adjusted, he made out the bed and the figure sleeping in it. "Ash," he said again, and crossed the room to lean down and grasp Ash's shoulder.

An instant later, there was a hand around his throat, a very small compact laser pointed at his face, and a pair of eyes so dark they were nearly black staring into his own, no recognition behind them.

Temple froze, and then very carefully removed his hand from Ash's shoulder.

The other man blinked, seeming to come back to himself. "… Temple?" he asked. He took a breath and lowered the gun, sticking it back beneath his pillow and releasing his grip on Temple's neck. "What the hell, man? What time is it?"

The questions were delivered as though he hadn't just been a finger-twitch from drilling a neat hole through Temple's brain, and if Temple weren't so worried about Red right now he might've, y'know, *said something* about that.

But, he *was* worried about Red right now, so he only said, "I just fucked up really bad and it's all your fault, so come help me."

Ash stared at him. "*Standard*, Temple. Please use it. I also speak English and Vithii, if that helps."

Temple ground his teeth in frustration. "I couldn't sleep, so I went to the atrium to sit for a while. But Ryder was already there. We hung out for a bit, and I asked her why she couldn't sleep. She said, because of the past. So I asked her who Eldrin was—that's the name she was mumbling when she was delirious. Then, when she didn't answer, I asked if that was the name of the child who died." He paused. "You know about that part, right? About the charges against her?"

Ash ran a hand up his face and through his hair.

"Son of a scurvy bitch, Temple," he said. "Okay, so, bonus points for not beating around the bush, I suppose. Big penalty for lack of tact. Where is she?"

"She jumped up and nearly ran back inside, then she went in one of the bedrooms and locked the door."

"Wonderful," Ash muttered, and raised the light level in the room to something a little more usable.

Temple waited while Ash rummaged for a shirt and slid it on over his sleep pants, his eyes drawn to the vicious black and blue marks striping across the flat planes of his back. A frown furrowed Temple's face, but he was too distracted by the current crisis to comment. When Ash started pawing through a drawer in the battered desk in the corner, Temple said, "What are you doing? Come on—"

Ash came up with what looked like a metal paperclip and said, "Emergency lock pick. Right, let's go."

The trip back to Ryder's room seemed to take longer than the trip from it had, which was ridiculous. Temple couldn't even have said why he was so worried—there had just been something about her in that frozen moment before she bolted that made the fine hairs on his arms stand up.

He knocked softly on the door. "Red? I've got Ash with me. Please let us in."

There was no reply, and the knot of worry in his stomach grew tighter.

Ash sighed. "It's a mechanical lock, Ryder. That's almost insulting, you know. We're coming in, and if there are any deadly weapons pointed at us when we do, I'm going to be even more cross than I already am."

Hypocrite, Temple thought, but kept the sentiment to himself.

The hallway around them remained quiet. Ryder had apparently chosen a room as far as possible from the other occupied bedrooms. Ash muttered something uncomplimentary and leaned over the lock, pulling the bent paperclip out of his pocket. It was clear that the mechanical locks in the old house weren't even *good* mechanical locks, because it only took moments for the click of rotating tumblers to pierce the silence.

Ash opened the door and prowled inside. Temple followed and closed it behind him. He scanned the room and found Ryder sitting half-sideways in a threadbare, high-backed chair, staring at a small brown bottle with a white safety lid on the table next to her. She didn't speak or look at them. Temple crossed and grabbed the bottle, examining it in the low light. The label was for a popular brand of prescription sedatives, and the bottle was nearly full.

He turned an accusing gaze on the woman in the chair, real fear prickling at his heart.

"Ryder?" Ash prompted, more than a hint of worry beneath his cultured tones.

She narrowed her eyes at them, glaring first at Temple, and then at Ash. "Oh, be serious. If I wanted to commit suicide, I'd go outside with a blaster and blow a hole through my cerebellum."

Temple wasn't sure if that qualified as reassurance or not. "So what's with these?" he pressed. "Why are you eye-fucking a bottle of sedatives if you're so perfectly peachy?"

"*Tact*, Temple," Ash reminded.

Ryder continued to glare at him. "I want to sleep," she said very slowly and distinctly, as if to an imbecile. "That's what sedatives are for, in case it's escaped your attention. I was debating whether a higher dose would interfere with my REM cycles enough to let me have some *dreamless* sleep for a change."

———◆———

Ryder watched warily as Ash made himself comfortable on the edge of her rumpled bed, while Temple continued to loom over her. The last thing she wanted right now was an audience, but it was becoming painfully clear that what she wanted wasn't really a metric that interested the cosmos at large.

"Maybe you'd sleep easier if you got a few things off your chest, Ryder," Ash said. There was nothing in his voice to make it sound like an accusation, but that's how she heard it nonetheless.

"Tell me something, Ash," she said in an unnaturally flat voice. "You obviously found the charges and court documents when you were digging around under my real name, but you haven't told the others. Why not?"

Ash had the gall to look offended. "Of course I didn't tell the others. It wouldn't even occur to me unless the information became necessary to save your life, or the lives of others. Do you really see me in such a way that this would surprise you? It's not my story to tell, Ryder, and anyway, I don't have the facts."

"For what it's worth," Temple put in, "he's not lying. I grilled him yesterday about you, and aside from saying some nice and terribly vague things about you being a good person, he was as tight-lipped as a mollusk."

"'A good person'?" Ryder mocked. "That's disingenuous, even for you, Ash. If you saw the charges, then you already have all the facts you need."

"Not the real ones," Ash said, failing to rise to the bait.

"Those *are* the real facts!" Ryder snapped.

"Bullshit," Temple said, slamming the pill bottle down on the table. He turned, looking down at her as she sat hunched in the chair. She stayed there, pinned in place, unable to make herself surge to her feet and push him away. Instead, a huge mass of… something… was gathering in her chest, demanding release. Demanding to be heard.

"I performed unlicensed experiments on a two-year-old boy using nanobots, and he died! That's a fact!" she nearly growled in Temple's face.

"All right," came Ash's maddeningly calm voice from the bed, "You performed unlicensed experiments on a two-year-old boy and he died. Now tell us why."

She curled around herself, trying to hold everything in as her body started to shake, but it was too late. "Because he was my son, and I thought it might save him," she said miserably, her face crumpling as the years of repressed grief threatened to spill past her emotional armor.

Temple slid to his knees beside her chair. "Oh, Red," he murmured. "Fucking hell."

She covered her face with her hand.

"What was wrong with him?" Ash asked, his voice gone low and soothing.

Ryder remembered papers fluttering to the ground, printed with a genetic death sentence.

"Bendrit's syndrome," she said into her hand. "His cells stopped coding for the amino acid tartrathene."

"And that's fatal?" Temple asked, his hand coming to rest on her knee. Somehow, the small gesture made the rest of her protective walls crumble, and she nodded, her eyes squeezing closed.

"It's fatal within weeks once the changes in a child's body cause the gene to deactivate. It usually happens around eighteen to twenty months of age, but Eldrin had just celebrated his second name-day when he started showing symptoms."

She dragged in a painful breath, trying to stop her hands from trembling. "I was already a successful neurosurgeon, specializing in microsurgery and researching nanotech applications within the medical industry. When Eldrin got sick, I immediately dug up every paper and study that had ever been done on Bendrit's. But there was nothing useful. The disease has a one-hundred-percent fatality rate. Without tartrathene, the skin becomes hopelessly delicate, the lightest brush enough to injure and scar."

Temple winced, his hand squeezing her leg.

"It's a horrible death," she said blankly. "Infection, uncontrollable bleeding, continuous, intractable pain. Jodor—my bondmate—was nearly frantic when we got the results of the genetic tests and the final diagnosis. We both were. He blamed me for passing on damaged genes. Told me that I was a doctor, and that I needed to fix it, no matter what it took. I'd been working on a side project using military-grade nanotech to rewrite the genes inside cancerous tumors in vitro, and… I thought…"

Ash made a pained noise. "You thought maybe you could rewrite your son's genetic code, using bots. Gods… *Ryder*."

SIXTEEN

Ryder nodded. "I knew there was no way in the world that the medical board would sign off. And even if they had, the red tape would have tied up the research for months. Years."

"And you only had weeks." Temple's voice was raspy.

"Yes. I still had access to the stock of nanotech from the cancer project. I stole a sample and started work in secret to train the bots to rewrite the code for tartrathene." She swallowed hard. "I worked nearly around the clock for weeks, watching Eldrin get worse day by day. As soon as I had bots that could make living cells produce the amino acid in vitro, I engineered some Vitharan *b'laat* flies to test. There was no time to engineer anything larger like rodents or *feldeh* beasts."

"You would have had to alter the fertilized ova and wait for the embryos to mature and be born," Ash said, "and it would have been too late."

She nodded, straightening in the chair—her eyes unfocused as the past played out like a holovid in front of her. "He was so weak. So delicate. He'd been in full quarantine since the diagnosis, to help stave off infection. But every time the nurses changed the dressings on his arms and legs, I was terrified that some pathogen would find its way inside him."

Temple was still kneeling at her feet, his hand on her leg a grounding sensation. "So, the bots worked on the *b'laat* flies, and…?"

She swallowed hard, feeling like the lump in her throat was choking her. "I injected him without telling anyone. Even a simple hypo-injector was enough to leave this… horrible hematoma at the injection site. He was wrapped up in bandages from head to toe, to keep him from touching anything. I couldn't hold him. I couldn't…"

She trailed off.

"What happened then, Ryder?" Temple asked.

She shook her head slowly, remembering the ever-accelerating slide into disaster over the following weeks. If the humans' hell was a real place, she'd seen a glimpse of it during that dark and hopeless time.

"For a few days, nothing," she said. "Then, the skin on his chest and stomach started to heal. It wasn't much, at first. Just places where the scrapes and pressure damage began to scab over, rather than continuously oozing pus. The other doctors were bewildered. Bendrit's doesn't *improve*. It just gets worse and worse until the patient dies."

"Did they realize what you'd done?" Ash asked.

Ryder shook her head. "Not immediately. It's a rare enough condition that they thought he might simply be an exceptional case. For a little over a week, he continued to improve incrementally. Until, one day, he had a massive immune reaction, and they couldn't find the cause."

"Because of the bots?" Temple hazarded.

"Yes. Because I'd made a mistake. Eldrin was already on a regimen of bio-therapeutics intended to regulate his immune response against any pathogens he was exposed to. One of the possible side effects of those kinds of drugs is an inflammatory cascade effect, where the immune cells overreact to a perceived threat and respond so violently that healthy tissues are damaged as a result. The sudden influx of bots triggered such a response, which grew invisibly until it reached a sort of tipping point where his body started attacking itself."

"And the other doctors still didn't know why?" Ash questioned.

"They did. I told them as soon as I saw what was happening." That had been the moment Ryder first experienced what it was like to become an outcast, rejected by her peers. "I was immediately placed on administrative leave; only allowed supervised visitation of my son with two or more security personnel present."

Temple looked up at her with dark eyes. "And… Eldrin?"

"They managed to keep him alive for three more weeks. The treatments they used to try and control the immune cascade interfered with the more effective classes of painkillers, and he cried constantly because it hurt so much." Her voice was faint. Far away. "Parts of his body continued to show improvement in skin quality and resilience, while other parts never did. Eventually, he slipped into a coma and died of multiple organ failure."

"I'm so sorry, Red," Temple told her, but the words slipped over her without penetrating the scars of untouched grief.

"And where was your bondmate during all of this?" Ash asked. "Where was Jodor Erisuel?"

A thin thread of bitter anger wove through Ryder's numbness.

"He was living his life. Climbing his ladder through Party ranks, accepting the heartfelt handshakes and back-pats from his fellow politicians, all of them *so terribly sorry* to hear about what he was going through. At least, they were sorry until they found out about the scandal involving his bondmate who had broken the law and experimented on his son using restricted nanotech. As soon as the clouds of scandal started to form around him, he distanced himself from me. The day after Eldrin died, he renounced me and threw me out of our house."

Temple's grip on her knee tightened until it was almost painful. "He dumped you *the day after your son died*?"

She blew out a breath. "He did. I hid out in a hotel room for more than a week, but either Jodor or the hospital had been busy behind the scenes. I was summarily fired and my medical credentials stripped. Law enforcement got involved and froze access to my bank accounts. Then, as soon as I was conveniently at rock bottom, I got a message from Jodor, telling me to meet him behind a club in the Central District. Fool that I was, I thought maybe he'd rethought things and realized that we needed to face this together. Fuck, what an idiot I was back then."

"What did he do?" Ash asked quietly.

"He lured me into an alley and tried to have me killed. He'd hired two thugs to grab me and make it look like a suicide. I got free and fled into the undercity. With no other options that I could see, I set up as a back alley, no-questions-asked medical practitioner, and stayed there until I met Kade a couple of years later. You know the rest."

With a jolt of shock, she realized that she'd just told these two men her complete story—the first time the words had ever passed her lips to another living soul. And… they were both still here. Ash still sat on the edge of her bed, looking down at his clasped hands. Temple still knelt at her feet, the hand that had clutched her knee gentling as the last words faded away.

Temple raised his eyes, anger behind them. Before she could wonder if it was directed at her, he said, "You should have killed him when you had a blaster in your hand and he was lying unconscious at your feet."

She shook her head. "And become known as the woman who murdered both her child *and* her bondmate? No, thank you."

Ash breathed out harshly and looked up. "Ryder, look at me." She did, reluctantly. "You did not murder your son. You attempted a radical and experimental treatment of a terminal disease—and, yes, it was an illegal treatment. It didn't work, but it might have. You are guilty of violating whatever statutes deal with medical research and the regulation of nanotech. You are not guilty of murder. Ask me sometime what crimes *I'm* guilty of committing. Ask Kade. Ask Draven or Hunter."

"Fucking *Jodor* was almost guilty of murder," Temple muttered. "I can't believe I had a chance to take his ass out, and I blew it. No offense, but your ex is a real bastard, Red."

It was surreal, sitting here and listening to these two human men talking to her like this. But… they were human, and perhaps that went a long way toward explaining why there were still large parts of her story that they didn't understand. For some reason, now that so much of her hidden past had already been laid bare, she felt the strong urge to explain the rest—to just… put it all out there, and finally be done with it.

"It's more complicated than that," she said tiredly, giving in to the strange compulsion to un-burden herself.

Ash tilted his head. "I know you *think* it's more complicated than that, but I assure you, it really isn't."

She looked down, and very deliberately moved her knee away from Temple's light grip. His hand slid away, and he took the hint, scooting back to sit on the floor with his back braced against the side of the bed frame, a little way from where Ash was perched.

She took a deep breath, trying to decide the best way to explain something so fundamentally Vithii to a pair of human men.

"You call Jodor my *ex*, like we're a couple of humans who got a divorce or an annulment or something. But that's not the way Vithii mating bonds work. He might want me dead and I may wish that I'd never met him… but I'm still his bondmate. We're still mated."

Ash was silent, waiting for her to continue, but Temple bristled.

"*Bullshit*," he said. "He doesn't get to claim you that way after he threw you away like trash when you needed him the most. Fuck him."

Her throat ached, on hearing someone else so concisely describe the ways in which she'd been hurt and discarded.

"He doesn't have to claim it," she managed. "It's a simple biological fact, and I wear it like a tattoo, for every other Vithii on Ilarius to see."

"I don't understand," Temple said.

She closed her eyes, and then opened them again, staring at the dimly lit ceiling with its cracked plaster and mold stains.

"That's because you're human," she said. "You're human, and you don't know what it means to be *grei'kaapt*."

SEVENTEEN

"In fact," Ash said, "I do know what it means to be *grei'kaapt*, Ryder. And while, as a human, I can't and don't claim to have firsthand experience with that particular little socio-cultural gem, I assure you I'm painfully familiar with the ways in which both humans and Vithii like to twist biology into something society can use as a weapon against the innocent."

"Well, one of you two had better clue me in," Temple said, frowning, "because I have no idea what you're talking about."

Ryder sighed and let herself fall into the comforting role of physician, well aware of the irony. She'd always found the way Vithii guarded the details of their biology and mating rituals intensely irritating, as though educating themselves and the humans with whom they shared this colony planet was some sort of threat to the natural order of things.

Well, fuck 'em. What were they going to do, make her *more* of an outcast for daring to explain the details of how biology had screwed over her life?

"The Vithii bonding ritual isn't a ceremony, like a human marriage is," she began. "It's a biological coupling—although most couples do, in fact, have a ceremony in conjunction with it, to publicly record the details of the joining. But in the absence of any such record, there's not a Vithii alive who couldn't determine if a couple were bonded or not within moments of coming within smelling distance."

Temple lifted an eyebrow.

"Even if you blindfold them, Vithii can tell if another Vithii is male or female, single or bonded," she continued. "Or… if they're *grei'kaapt*."

"I have actually heard the word a few times," Temple said, "though I'll admit I didn't give it much thought. From the context, I took it to mean divorced, or maybe widowed."

"Vithii don't divorce," Ash said.

"Vithii *can't* divorce," Ryder corrected. "And the word *grei'kaapt* can only apply to females. It refers to a female whose mate has either died or abandoned her."

Temple looked at her in confusion. "And other Vithii can somehow smell this on you? *How*?"

"Pheromones," she said. "Vithii can and do have sex without forming a mating bond. But once the male bites the mating gland at the base of the female's neck while knotting her during intercourse, his saliva stimulates her endocrine system to produce the pheromones that tell other Vithii, 'I'm mated.' That pheromone kills arousal in other males and engenders feelings of respect and protectiveness toward the female instead."

"Okay," Temple said, "I suppose that's a neat bit of evolutionary biology, and I can see why it would make it difficult for a Vithii woman to find a new partner if her old partner left, but—"

She cut him off. "Without regular contact with her mate—specifically, without his saliva stimulating her mating gland, that pheromone changes. Instead of saying, 'I'm mated,' it says, 'I'm mated, but my mate either died or rejected me.' As you might guess, that pheromone has a rather different effect on aroused Vithii males."

Temple still appeared bewildered. "Like…what kind of effect?"

"Disgust, mostly," Ryder said in a completely flat tone. "Sometimes anger. In Vithii past childbearing age, it's a fairly weak response, since all pheromone production reduces sharply with age. In younger Vithii, though, it's an evolutionary avoidance tactic, steering males away from females that are undesirable for some reason."

"That's…" Temple started, only to trail off. "Okay, sorry, I actually don't know what to say to that right now."

Ryder shrugged. "There are some hormonal therapies that mask the effects to varying degrees, but they tend to be expensive, and the efficacy fades over time. A lot of women have the gland surgically removed, but it's still obvious to other Vithii what's been done and why. There's a whole other load of prejudices centered around that practice."

"And the men?" Temple asked, sounding decidedly shell-shocked. "Aren't they giving off some sort of 'I fucked over my wife' vibe?"

Ryder's snort was bitter. "Males give off mating markers even after they've renounced a bonded partner. But, biologically, there's nothing to stop them mating another female if one's stupid enough to let them near her gland. Like I said, a male can't be *grei'kaapt*; only a female. Socially, multiple matings are frowned on, though. You can't record one unless you're willing to commit fraud."

Temple was on his feet now, pacing. "That is beyond fucked up." He paused. "Red, don't take this the wrong way, but your species is *whacked*." He scrubbed a hand roughly over his face in agitation. "And my sister married one of these guys…"

Ryder wrapped her arms around herself, feeling strangely chilled despite the balmy late-summer night. "If it helps, even though they had a bonding ceremony, Hunter and Skye can never mate in the way that two Vithii mate each other. The biology doesn't work that way."

"There's also the small matter of Hunter not being a callous bastard," Ash put in. "Please believe me when I say, Skye could do a lot worse."

"Seriously, though," Ryder said, still feeling cold and oddly detached from her surroundings, "she's human. If he left her, it might break her heart, but it wouldn't leave her *grei'kaapt*. It wouldn't leave her… untouchable."

Temple, who had been pacing again, stopped, looking at her oddly. Ash was also staring at her, but there was an expression of slow-dawning realization on his face that she didn't understand.

"Is that how you feel, Ryder?" Ash asked carefully. "Untouchable? You shouldn't, you know."

She shivered and pinned him with a glare, which he ignored. "Shouldn't I, *leetha*? And just how often have you seen a member of my own species touch me, or allow my touch outside of a medical setting?"

Ash shook his head slowly back and forth, once. He got up and crossed to her chair, not even hesitating as he stepped into her personal space and pulled her upper body against him, wrapping one arm around her and cupping the back of her head with the other, all without a word.

Ryder froze, her mind a complete blank. While not as tall as either her or Temple, Ash was still reasonably tall for a human. Seated, her head hit him mid-chest, her cheek settling naturally into the space beneath his collarbone. His other hand slid down to encircle her shoulders, being careful of her wound but nonetheless squeezing with steady pressure.

No one had held her like this in years, and she didn't know how to respond. She sat doll-like, her arms unmoving, unable to bridge the gap between the reality inside her head and whatever Ash was doing, holding her like he didn't care that she was broken and tainted… like he was trying to prove a point or something.

"Ryder," he said, "if the others don't touch you, it's because they're afraid of being summarily castrated the moment they try it. You carry around an invisible force field the size of a small moon, you know."

She closed her eyes tightly, aware that her breathing was doing something strange inside her chest.

"Do the Vithii here desire you?" Ash continued. "No, it's true. They don't. But every damned person in this house cares deeply for your prickly, short-tempered arse." His tone changed, softening with amusement or humor. "Including the person in this room who's been staring at you like a lovesick puppy since more or less the first moment I met him."

"The one who's seriously considering dragging your skinny British ass off her so he can have a go, you mean?" Temple asked, his voice nearly a growl.

Ryder felt Ash's chest move against her cheek, a silent laugh. "That's him, yes." He gave her a final squeeze, and she managed to drag one arm free of her paralysis just long enough to cup his elbow in her hand as he pulled away.

Ash gave her a lopsided smile. "Alas, I can see I won't be the one to really convince you. I suppose I'll have to leave you in more capable hands." He reached down and snatched the pill bottle from beside her, shaking two doses onto the table and recapping it before sliding it into his pocket. "Now, you two, it's late, and I expect you to either talk, shag, or get some damned rest."

He rounded on Temple, pointing at his chest. "Before I leave, though… *you*. Don't ever fucking touch me without warning again when I'm asleep." His finger moved toward Ryder. "And *you*. If you're to lock yourself in a room with a bottle of sedatives, at least choose a door with a decent lock. Goodnight, and I don't want to see either of you again until I've had a solid eight cycles of sleep."

A moment later, the door closed behind him, leaving the room in silence so complete it almost seemed to echo, stretching out as Ryder's heartbeat pulsed against her chest.

"Is he always like that?" Temple asked eventually.

Ryder tried to shake herself free of… whatever the fuck had just happened in here. "Not… always?" she said. Which sounded better than saying, *I have literally no idea what that was or what I'm supposed to do about it.*

Temple heaved a breath. "Right. Next question. How worried should I be about the fact that you've just spilled your guts regarding some staggeringly painful subjects, and you're just kind of… sitting there? Because if you were human, I would find that worrying, but you're not human, and I don't really know how Vithii normally react to something like that, and… now I'm babbling." He ruffled his short dreadlocks, and muttered, "Prophets, I should have let Ash shoot me after I woke him up."

"Considering what we just went through to get you out of that prison, I'm glad you didn't," Ryder said. "Though, to answer your question, I'm not sure. I don't really have that strong a background in psychology. I was a neurosurgeon."

He nodded slowly. "Maybe we should just agree that of the three options we've been presented, sleep sounds like the one least likely to get us into further trouble tonight?"

She studied him, tracing his finely sculpted human facial features. "You don't have to stay, you know."

He stared right back at her. "Okay, the answer to that is twofold. First, I *want* to stay. And second, I wouldn't put it past Ash to have booby-trapped the damned door. So, sleep—yes or no? I don't know about you, but I'm fucking knackered."

She thought of all the times in the past few years when circumstances had forced her to sleep in the same room as someone she trusted. How it always made her feel safer. More at ease, knowing another person was there to watch her back. Of course, it also made her feel guilty, as though she were forcing her *grei'kaapt* presence on the others in a context that had an inherent sort of intimacy to it.

But Temple had made it clear that he didn't find her nearness distasteful. He'd been positively bewildered by the entire concept. He was human. Her pheromones were meaningless background noise to him, neither pleasant nor unpleasant. He wanted to be here; she wasn't imposing on him.

"Yes," she said. "Sleep sounds… good. I'm fine here in the chair if you want to take the—"

A hand grasped her left forearm and pulled her to her feet.

"Gods above, you are hard-headed," Temple said, as he dragged her into his arms and slanted his lips across hers—another human kiss, like the one he'd surprised her with when she'd awoken in the medical room to find him and Skye sitting with her.

Maybe she should start examining the reason why she was still surprised?

As before, it was unfamiliar… strange… alien… intimate. Her skin felt tight and hot from the sudden overload of touching; first Ash's platonic embrace, and now this unexpected shock of—what? Her earlier chill was melting away, the warmth of skin on skin driving it back, pushing it away. She still had no idea what she was supposed to do with this odd slide of lips on lips.

She also didn't want it to stop.

It did, though, after an interlude of a minute or two—whether because she wasn't responding correctly or because Temple felt he'd made his point, she didn't know. He slid his cheek along hers until his full lips were at her ear.

"Sorry," he whispered, the movement of air against sensitive nerves making her shiver. "I know that's not a Vithii thing, but I'm still half-convinced that if I dragged your head to one side and buried my teeth in your neck, you'd snap me in two."

The strangest feeling twisted in her belly at the sound of his words, a sensation so unfamiliar after eight long years that she couldn't quite credit it as being real. Words slipped past her lips without thought, shocking her as she heard herself utter them.

"Only one way to find out..."

Temple groaned, and pressed his face against the same area he'd threatened to bite. She realized that her hands had come up to wrap around his corded biceps.

"Prophets, don't tempt me," he muttered, before straightening to brush a final kiss across her lips and pull away. "Seriously. Tell me that again in the morning, and I can guarantee you'll get a different response. But... a lot of heavy shit went down tonight, and despite what your crazy-ass friend seems to think, I'm not sure a poorly negotiated interspecies shag between two exhausted people is the logical response. So... sleep?"

"Sleep," she agreed faintly, still stuck on the part where she was *grei'kaapt*, and a man needed to talk himself out of having sex with her. Because... well... *what*?

"Good," Temple said, and handed her one of the sedative doses.

She took it without hesitation, knowing that after the last couple of hours, her chances of doing anything other than lying there dissecting every word that had been spoken and every gesture that had been made was essentially nil. The blasted pills weren't a long-term solution or even a medium-term one, but she figured at this point, the universe owed her a few uninterrupted cycles of sleep.

She nodded toward a bottle of water on the bedside table when Temple picked up the other dose and looked around. He washed his down with a couple of mouthfuls, and she swallowed hers dry.

"Bloody hell, I needed this," he said as he flopped onto the mattress and scooted back to the wall, making space for her.

"Needed what?" she asked, still feeling thrown by the whole situation, teetering between accepting it and expecting someone to burst in and deliver the punch line to the practical joke.

"Someone to hold," he said simply and lifted an arm, inviting her to come and lie down underneath it.

Ryder hesitated for another instant before deciding it was past time to say *fuck it*, and sliding into the bed. She settled on her side, facing away, lying stiff and unsure.

"Hard-headed," Temple murmured again, before he cinched an arm around her waist and dragged her backwards into a more comfortable position with him spooning her from behind.

Her heart pounded a flustered rhythm that he surely must have been able to feel, given how close they were. It was no match for her traitorous muscles, though, which gradually softened and relaxed into the warm, protective embrace of someone she trusted. Watching her back? Prophets, he wasn't just *watching* it, he was draped over it like a sheltering cloak. No one was getting anywhere near her back without going through him first. His breath tickled her shoulder blade in slow, even puffs.

How had she survived without this for so long? Even when she'd been with Jodor, she'd never truly had anything like this. She'd thought she'd known intimacy, fool that she was, but all she'd known was duty and keeping up appearances. Now that she was here on the bed with Temple, she'd changed her mind—sleep was the last thing she wanted if it stole away her awareness of this feeling.

It was too late, though. The sedative was kicking in, only this time she was sliding down into the depths of oblivion with a blanket of comfort and security wrapped around her shoulders, rather than a sense of sinking dread. Maybe she'd been wrong… maybe she could have sleep and have this feeling at the same time.

Because that? Would be wonderful right about now.

EIGHTEEN

She awoke what seemed like a very long time later. Ryder had always been a light sleeper, prone to insomnia and quick to wake. In the medical profession, it wasn't a bad problem to have. Even with a sedative involved, though, it was disconcerting to come back to awareness and discover that the sun was not only up, it was way, *way* up.

The other reason behind her uncharacteristic stint of blissful unconsciousness was still pressed up against her back. He snored, evidently—a soft, deep rasp that somehow made her want to close her eyes again and join him once more in oblivion, despite the fact that they'd already slept half the night and half the day away.

Instead, she stretched, being careful of her healing shoulder. Her muscles pulled deliciously, and she realized how long it had been since she'd truly felt *rested*. The movement roused Temple, not to full wakefulness, but to a lighter state of half-awareness. His arm tightened around her and his body stretched as well, following her lead. Soft lips nuzzled the line of her scapula, as a hard length pressed against her ass through two sets of sleep pants.

Her mating gland gave a little tingling throb, echoed by the hot pulsing need that took up residence between her legs. She caught her breath in an involuntary gasp. Behind her, Temple went still, and she knew that he was properly awake.

"Good morning," he rasped, propping himself on an elbow. "I'd, uh, apologize for rutting on you, but I really hope I won't need to."

She craned around carefully, not wanting to twist her shoulder. Meeting his dark, liquid eyes, heavy and half-lidded with sleep, she took a slow breath… and let herself fall.

"Like I told you last night," she whispered, "I guess there's only one way to find out, isn't there?"

He shifted so she could roll onto her back, looking up at him. "You know, I've only just woken up," he said, a smile tugging one corner of his full lips, "and you've already made my day. Too bad I have absolutely no idea what I'm doing when it comes to Vithii sex. If we're really going to do this, would you care to offer any pointers?"

His hand was trailing up her side in a manner that was thoroughly distracting, but she made herself run through what she knew of human sexual practices and comparative anatomy. It was surprisingly difficult with her body yearning toward the promise of touch like a flower turning toward the sun.

"Uh, you'll need lube," she said, wincing internally at the decidedly unsexy pronouncement. "Human females self-lubricate, but for Vithii it's the males who produce slick when they're aroused." She cast around, and her eyes landed on the jar of moisturizing ointment she'd been using on the scar from her stab wound. "What's in there will work."

"Okay, good to know," he said, still stroking his hand over her waist and hip. His movements stilled, and his smile grew rueful. "Now, the question no human wants to ask. Is sex with a human going to be any good for you whatsoever? Vithii are tight-lipped about the subject, but there's still plenty of talk in human circles about Vithii males and their… endowments. If this is going to be a non-starter, you might as well let me down easy, Red."

Ryder shook her head. "Considering the fact that no one has touched me for the purpose of giving pleasure in years, I don't think you have to worry much about earning a gold medal in the interspecies sex Olympics, Temple."

He laughed aloud, a low, male noise that made the blood thrum even faster beneath her skin.

She swallowed. "To answer your question, though, Vithii sex might start with foreplay, or not. After penetration, the male ruts for a couple of minutes, usually triggering orgasm in both partners. Orgasm stimulates the male's penile knot to engorge, at the same time the female's vaginal sphincter contracts, locking them together. The female enters a coital trance for the duration of knotting, while endorphins flood the male's body, producing feelings of connection and protectiveness. It's sort of a cliché that Vithii males run their mouths during knotting, like their brain-to-mouth filter stops working when they've got their dicks inside someone."

Temple snickered into her shoulder. "Sorry… sorry. Is it only humans who find talking about the mechanics of sex to be inherently funny?" He dragged himself back to the appearance of seriousness, at least. "All right. So, basically, I can't knot you, and that may or may not interfere with your enjoyment of the… coital trance?"

She shrugged. "Detailed research is obviously needed. I'm volunteering for the initial study."

He grinned again. "Ooh… the scientific method. Sexy. Talk dirty to me, Red."

Her lips were trying to twist into some sort of unfamiliar shape. She was concerned that it might be a stupid, sappy smile of some kind. "I feel like you're not treating this subject with the gravity it deserves," she accused.

"Oh, believe me. I am," he said, still grinning. "How long does knotting usually last?"

"Variable. Half a cycle to two cycles, generally."

Temple nodded. "And the coital trance?"

"The same. The knot softens and the vaginal ring relaxes, at which point the male can withdraw." Ryder blinked up at him, wanting to be very clear about her expectations. "And none of this matters, really. I just want to touch you, and be touched by you. It's been… a very long time."

His smile softened, became hopelessly fond. "Believe me, Red, that part is not going to be a problem at all."

With that, he leaned down and kissed her again, human style. She closed her eyes, still not sold on the practice's value as sexual foreplay, but not about to complain. That lasted until his teeth closed around her lower lip, nipping sharply. Electricity shot down her spine, making her nipples harden as it passed, and she made a low noise into the kiss, bucking up instinctively.

He dragged her lip back, letting it slide through his teeth until it popped free, tingling. She lay there panting for a moment, staring at him, then grabbed his shoulders, dragging him back down for a rematch. Suddenly, what had been a strange, awkward brush of body parts became a contest as she strove to catch the tender flesh of his lips and mark it, while he did the same to her.

By the time he pulled away in favor of biting his way down her neck, her lips felt bruised and swollen, pulsing in time with the blood rushing through her mating gland and her sex.

"*Fuck*, Ryder," he groaned against her skin as his hand slid under the hem of her sleep shirt, his fingers splayed as he dragged them up to cup her left breast. "Clothes. Off." Two fingers pinched her nipple, and she arched into the sensation.

He let her go and knelt over her, dragging his shirt off to reveal sleek human musculature. The weeks he'd spent in prison had starved every ounce of fat from his body, and Ryder couldn't help thinking that her human anatomy class would have been a lot less boring if she'd had him available as a study aid.

She tried to peel her own shirt off, cursing as her shoulder protested.

"Let me," Temple murmured, sliding his hands up her sides, gathering the material as he went and slipping it over her head. Ryder's skin felt hot where his palms had skimmed it. "*Prophets*, you are gorgeous." Lips and teeth grazed her collarbone. "Strong." He nipped the top of her breast. "Beautiful." His tongue laved a spiral around her nipple. "*Sexy*." Teeth closed around the pebbled tip, and she cried out.

He sucked hard, nearly making her arch off the bed before he let go and she fell back, gasping. Not giving her time to recover, he grasped the loose elastic of her sleep bottoms and slid them down over the lean lines of her hips, tossing them aside. Immediately afterward, he slid out of the bed so he could follow suit, baring himself to her gaze.

He really was a work of art—his skin a dark shade not seen among Vithii. He had a tattoo of a snake eating its own tail circling the jut of his right hipbone, and the pink scar from his healing blaster burn was still starkly visible. A less obvious scar marked the place on his chest where he'd been shivved, the wound Ryder had been treating when the guards in the prison had come for her.

Who would have imagined that a few short days later, she would be fantasizing about running her tongue over that thin line, to see if it tasted any different than the rest of him?

A slow smile spread over his features as he saw her staring, and he crawled onto the foot of the bed, taking her leg in his hand and fastening lips and teeth to the inside of her knee, sucking the blood to the surface as she writhed. He pulled away with a pop and looked up the length of her body.

"I hope you don't mind marks," he said, "because you're going to be fucking covered in them by the time we're done."

The connection between her brain and her mouth short-circuited for a minute before she managed to croak, "Promises, promises."

He smirked and continued up her leg, leaving a trail of love bites as he went. By the time he reached her center, she was a sweating, trembling mess.

"Just remember," she threatened weakly. "I was a doctor, and I can come up with the kind of revenge that will leave you walking funny for a *week*."

"Mm-hmm. Promises, promises," he echoed, and lowered his mouth to her sex.

His lips and tongue explored her folds, focusing on an area a couple of centimeters away from where she really wanted him before he lifted his head and raised an eyebrow at her. "Okay, something's missing. Road map for the clueless human, please?"

She couldn't help it—she laughed, feeling lightheaded and strangely carefree. "Anterior vaginal wall, slightly less than a centimeter inside. Sorry, I forgot about that particular quirk of human anatomy."

"Inside, eh? Holy shit. I know a bunch of human women who would be insanely jealous right about now."

She mock glared at him, still fighting laughter. "Do I look like I want to hear about all the human women you know?"

"Ooh, touché," he said. "Let me see if I can make it up to you?"

With that, he lowered his head again, his soft human tongue delving over her entrance, curling a bit deeper each time, the sensation making her melt from the inside out. Without conscious thought, her hands found the soft, springy dreadlocks covering his head, fingers twining to keep him in place. He groaned, low and guttural, pressing her leg to the side to open her up so he could slide his tongue deeper.

His hands moved to cup her buttocks, one finger moving to tickle the pucker hidden between them, brushing lightly. Ryder went limp, small, needy sounds jerking free from her lips as he teased and licked. Within minutes, she shuddered as a swell of lazy pleasure washed outward from the point of contact. She moaned, long-unused muscles fluttering as her sleeping nerves awoke from hibernation.

He soothed her with shallower strokes of his tongue until she stilled, and lifted his head, large hands kneading her flesh. "More?" he asked.

"Fuck me," she demanded, not caring if it didn't end up being perfect, or if their bodies didn't fit together in the same way that two Vithii would. She needed him closer. She needed him *inside*.

"You don't need to tell me twice," he promised, crawling up to straddle her so he could reach for the jar of ointment she'd indicated earlier. He was fully hard, thicker and longer than she might have expected. His human erection was strangely static compared to what she was used to—unmoving except for the occasional twitch. Curious, she ran a finger along the underside, and it jumped.

Temple made a low noise in his throat and offered her the open jar. "Do the honors?" he asked.

She scooped up greasy ointment with two fingers, and he set the jar aside. His eyes slid closed as she smoothed it over the hard flesh, his head rolling back.

"Mmm... damn, that's good, Red," he said, his voice falling into a lower register. "In fact, that's so good you'd probably better stop now."

His hands played over her breasts, kneading them and tweaking the points. She reluctantly took her hand away, wiping it on the sheets to clean off the slippery ointment.

"I want to try something," he said. "No idea how well it'll work. Research, right?"

"Research is very important," she agreed.

"Anyway, I want to try taking you on your side from behind, if that's all right. And don't worry if I don't come when you do. I'm going to try not to, because once I do, that will pretty much be it. But don't worry, I have a *theory*."

Somehow, he managed to make the word sound completely filthy, and she huffed in amusement. "More dirty talk?" she teased. "Take me any way you like. Just *fucking take me*."

"Yes, *ma'am*," he agreed easily, and arranged them on their sides in more or less the same position they'd slept in earlier. "Shoulder all right?"

"What shoulder?" she asked scooting her hips back to meet him. "I can't even feel it right now…"

He ran a hand down her spine and back up, intensifying the melting, unraveling feeling inside her. At the top of the upstroke, his fingers brushed over the tight, irritated knot of her mating gland, a scarred and twisted thing since the one who had claimed her had abandoned it. The small, high-pitched cry that emerged in response to the unexpected contact was completely beyond her control.

Temple went very still. "Shit… Ryder, is that another injury? I'm sorry—"

"It's not a wound," she whispered, although maybe that was a lie. All right, it was *definitely* a lie. "It's my mating gland."

He was still frozen behind her. "Should I stay away from it? Does it hurt?"

A band tightened around her chest unexpectedly. "Only when you're not touching it," she breathed.

A sharp puff of air tickled her back, as though it had been punched from him. "*Fucking prophets*, Red. You're killing me." His forehead rested against the back of her neck for a beat. He pulled away moving to speak into her ear instead, his voice lowering to a growl. "I can't go back to the prison and tear that bastard apart with my bare hands, much as I might like to. But even if that waste of air is still out there breathing somewhere... tonight, this part of you is *mine*."

His palm rested over the reddened bump and she writhed, arching her back and trying to get him inside her as all rational thought fled. He lined up their hips and pressed in, the angle making the head of his cock slide over her clit as he thrust deeper. At the same time, he moaned and pressed his lips over her gland, biting down and tonguing it.

He probably had no idea of the symbolism involved in what he was doing. He *surely* had no idea that if a Vithii besides Jodor had dared do such a thing, they would almost certainly both be retching and bolting for opposite sides of the room within moments, as her body rejected the mismatched mating markers and started pouring out defensive pheromones.

But Ryder's endocrine system didn't recognize anything about Temple's human saliva, one way or the other. It was just meaningless chemicals, no different than standing outside in the rain.

Her body and mind, on the other hand, recognized the gesture for what it was. Claiming. Marking. Joining.

Everything she'd been desperate to have for eight long, painful years. She cried out in ecstasy, not caring who might be around to hear it. Not caring about anything except the press of teeth and tongue against needy flesh, and the slide of a hard cock against the bundle of nerves hidden inside her passage.

Temple bit down, holding her in place like a predator grasping its prize as he fucked into her. A low growl escaped him, and she was coming, jerking around him as the room around her whited out. As she gradually stilled, the press of teeth receded, replaced once more by the slow slide of a tongue, soothing.

Ryder gave a weak, needy whimper, and surrendered herself to the care of a lover for the first time since her mate had abandoned her. With a feeling of relief so profound it made her dizzy, she slid into the coital trance, the tight ring of muscle at her core clamping around Temple's cock to hold him inside her.

NINETEEN

Temple panted fast and hard against the skin of Ryder's neck, trying desperately not to come as her muscles rippled around him, milking his cock and begging him to spill inside her.

Not yet, he told himself. *Not yet.*

Prophets… her reaction to his lips and teeth on this strange, alien part of her… it made him want to tie her up so tight she could barely wriggle and tease it with slow flicks of his tongue for *hours*. Which… yeah. That image wasn't really helping him hold back from blowing his load as far inside her body as he could get.

Gradually, she settled, her orgasm subsiding, and he soothed the coppery knot of flesh with the flat of his tongue. Then, she made a soft, desperate sound that flew straight toward the deepest caveman part of him and buried itself inside like an arrow. He'd never heard anyone make a sound like that before, much less when they were impaled on his cock with his teeth-marks indented in their neck. It didn't matter what Ryder needed at that moment. Whatever it was, he would slice off a limb and hand it to her if that was what it took to fulfill her need.

He wrapped his arm around her, holding her against him, and felt her muscles go soft and pliant. Every ounce of tension bled from her body, except for the place where they were joined. When he'd entered her, it hadn't been that much different than with a human woman. Now, though, a strong ring of muscle clamped down on the base of his cock.

He caught his breath. It was… a bit like being inside a partner when they came during anal. Only, instead of squeezing and releasing, Ryder's muscles clamped down on him and *held*. If he were Vithii, he guessed he'd be knotting her right now. He'd worried that without a knot, this whole thing wouldn't work for her at all, but the trusting weight pressed against him argued that it was working for her pretty damned well.

And, he couldn't lie—it might be frustrating as hell, but the natural cock ring squeezing the base of his shaft was working pretty fucking well for him, too. He'd played with rings on a few occasions, and for him, the net result was a long-lasting erection, extreme sensitivity, and the inability to come until it was removed.

So, an armful of warm, pliant Ryder, lying trusting in his embrace? With his cock trapped and oversensitive inside her for an undetermined amount of time before he could come? Yeah—that was definitely the kind of sexual torture he could get behind.

He wasn't sure how aware she was of her surroundings, but even if she couldn't feel it, he still wanted to touch her everywhere. He let his hand play over her full breasts, stroking, caressing, and cupping their solid weight. He splayed his palm over her ribs and stomach, sliding down to tease the place where they were joined. He pressed soft kisses to every part of her neck and back he could reach.

He'd thought Ryder was relaxed when she first entered the trance, but with each slow touch she seemed to melt into him more and more, until he could barely tell where she started and he ended. Only the occasional flutter of her passage around him marred her perfect stillness. The stimulation sending little lightning bolts of pleasure to coil in the base of his spine, building without an outlet.

He couldn't thrust, but he rolled his hips, teasing more little ripples from her passage. The whole thing was shockingly intense. Time started to run together under the onslaught of his body's growing desperation to come, the room around him falling away until it was just Ryder's body against his, holding him hostage, body and soul.

When she finally drew in a deep breath and stretched like an awakening sleeper, his breath hitched out as her muscles tightened around him and then began to ease.

"Oh, gods," he groaned. "Ryder, please... I need to move or I'll go mad."

When she made a sleepy noise and rocked her hips back, he nearly sobbed in relief. He arched his spine, draping himself over her back and sliding into her with slow, deep thrusts. She murmured something in Vithii, rolling her head to expose her neck. He took the invitation and clamped his lips over her mating gland, just as his long denied release slammed into him like a freighter crash.

He thought he cried out against her skin as his hips jerked into her, his seed spilling inside her warm depths as though it would never stop. His vision started to tunnel in from the sides, and he squeezed his eyes shut with a final rough grunt against the side of her neck.

When he was finally spent, Temple let his softening length slide free of her body, and just breathed. He sucked in deep drafts of air, feeling as though he'd just had every worry and dark thought circling in his head drawn out through his dick. The woman in his arms had exorcized all of it, down to the last tiny niggle, leaving him empty of everything except the sure and certain knowledge that he would never, ever let her go.

They lay side by side for a long time, no sounds breaking the room's stillness except for the twin rasp of their breathing, slow and deep.

"I don't care what anyone else says, or what they think," he told her eventually, his voice hoarse. "You're mine, and I'm yours. I'm not letting you go. Society can go fuck itself."

Ryder was quiet for a moment before she spoke.

"Temple… I can never bond with you. I can't even marry you. I'm already bonded," she said, and he *hated* the pain coloring her voice. Hated that her culture had beaten her down so far she couldn't hear what he was telling her, or share the soul-deep certainty that he felt right now.

He rolled onto an elbow and cupped her cheek, drawing her eyes up to meet his. "You're not hearing me, Red. What do I care about a piece of paper? I don't give a damn about an official bonding, or a marriage, or any of it. If a bonding sanctions the rights of a bastard who would abuse and abandon a woman after she gave herself to him like you just gave yourself to me, I don't want any part of it. I don't recognize your bonding to Jodor Erisuel. As far as I'm concerned, he no longer exists."

"I wish it were that easy," she whispered.

He shook his head. "I think it's precisely as easy or as difficult as we make it. What we have, right here, right now in this bed—we can have this tomorrow, and the next day, and all the days until we die. You have an idea inside you of what it means to be *grei'kaapt*. I bet it's been drilled into you since you were a child, hasn't it? But, here and now, with me, it's not real. It's not *real*, Ryder."

He stared into her brown eyes, studying the copper-gold highlights in their depths, willing her to believe.

"Promise me you'll let me prove it to you," he urged. "Promise me you'll take a chance on this. On *us*."

He held his breath as she lifted a hand to his face, mirroring him. "Temple," she said, "after all these years alone and miserable, do you really think I'd give this up without a fight?"

Relief coursed through him and he closed his eyes, tipping his head forward until their foreheads rested together.

◆

The following day, Temple sat in the atrium with Jonah. The others were preparing to pull up stakes and head for some distant safehouse—something Kade had arranged for them in the middle of nowhere on the southern continent. Temple had offered to help, but there wasn't really much here that needed to be packed. Hell, the only worldly goods *he* could lay claim to right now were a pair of battered scrubs.

It irked him that he couldn't retrieve anything from his former life, but he also understood the necessity of staying far away from anyplace the authorities might have under surveillance after his escape. Skye, he knew, had never been able to return to her apartment after she'd escaped from the Regime complex where their father had been held. They were both fugitives, cut off from their former lives as surely as if they'd died and been reborn as new people.

As a human prison escapee, Jonah was a fugitive as well, but not quite on the same level Temple, Skye, Ryder, Hunter, and the others currently occupied. Jonah was a nobody—a kid in a gang who been in the wrong place at the wrong time and gotten swept up in the Regime's net. The authorities might care about him in the sense that they cared about recapturing all of the other prisoners who'd managed to slip free during the riot, but they weren't going to devote significant time and resources specifically to track him down and nab him again.

Even so, Temple asked, "Are you sure you won't come with us, kid?"

"Nah," Jonah said. "I want to reconnect with my family. Try to get my life back on track and do something that'll make a difference. Kade and Ash set me up with a new identichip and e-records—I guess they're from some guy who died during the bio-attack."

Temple nodded. "You've got an aunt here in the Capital, right?"

"An aunt and uncle, yeah. They're good people. I can stay with them while I'm getting on my feet again. I gave Kade their comm code as a way to contact me, in case there's anything I can do for y'all in the future. Also, Ash said he'd be back here in the city before long and would check in from time to time."

"Take care of yourself, Jonah," Temple said, standing and pulling the younger man into a back-slapping embrace. "I'm afraid things are likely to get a hell of a lot worse before they get better."

Jonah laughed. "Oh, they're gonna get *better*? Well, I guess that's something to look forward to, then." He pulled away and sobered. "Seriously, though, don't worry about me, Temple. Worry about yourself, and Skye, and your new girlfriend. From what I've seen, whenever things go to hell, you're likely to be smack in the middle of it."

Temple snorted. "Yeah, I've got a feeling you're probably right about that."

* * *

The trip to the southern continent was a nerve-wracking one for Temple. Ash, who had been in and out over the previous few days, provided him with a small suitcase containing a couple changes of clothes, toiletries, fake identification, and a credit chip with a modest balance. The journey itself was accomplished in stages—first, ground transport to a private hangar, then a short hop on three separate ships to a larger terminal, and finally, the trans-oceanic leg on a commercial suborbital carrier.

Hunter and Pax were not with them. With Hunter's tattoos and Pax's implants, they were, quite simply, too recognizable. Skye had dyed her long hair brown, and Ryder, after promising Temple it would wash out in a few days, dyed hers black. Every time they came face to face with security, Temple had to make himself breath slowly and pray that the nervous sweat on his palms didn't give him away.

The others seemed, if not blasé, then at least confident. Temple wondered how many times they'd done this over the years—assuming new identities, slipping beneath the radar.

After the better part of a day spent traveling, they were met at the run-down terminal in Chell'ar by an equally run-down ground transport. The old truck looked like it was more often used to haul grain than tourists. Chell'ar was the largest city on the southern continent, which wasn't saying much. Aside from the terminal, it seemed to consist mostly of grain elevators, bars, and a handful of loan brokers.

The transport's driver was an elderly Vithii man, his white hair sticking out crazily from beneath a human-style billed cap. "Get in, get in," he said. "Kade, it's good to see you again, my boy. Hop in the cab. The rest of you will have to ride in the back."

Relieved beyond measure to be out from under the roving eye of security cameras and terminal guards, Temple jumped into the open bed of the transport and gave Ryder a hand up after him. The others followed, claiming spots along the slatted sides while Ryder leaned against his shoulder.

"Who's the old guy?" Temple asked over the rumble of the engine, once they were underway. "I'd assumed this place would be another abandoned property like the one in the Capital."

Draven answered. "Nah. The driver and his bondmate were friends of Kade's parents, back in the day. They were all active together in the opposition party. After the Premiere had Kade's parents offed, Kade helped get these two away to safety… out of the Capital and down here to the middle of nowhere. They owe him one, to put it mildly."

Temple supposed that *would* be a powerful motivator for helping someone out. He leaned back, enjoying the sight of the brilliant blue sky, the clean air, and the feeling of Ryder dozing against his chest. He wasn't fool enough to believe this would be a carefree vacation, but he hadn't been away from the congested grime and smog of the city since he was a kid on vacation with Skye and their parents. Damned if he wasn't going to enjoy the fresh air and sunshine while he could.

The drive from Chell'ar to wherever they were going took almost two cycles. When they arrived at a cheerful, sprawling farmhouse, it was to find two sleek black fighter jets parked in a nearby field. Skye's face lit up. She was out of the transport the instant it rolled to a halt, running across the grass to meet Hunter, who swept her into his strong arms and held her tight.

Temple tightened his arm around Ryder's shoulders, aware that a stupid grin was stealing across his face. Ryder groaned.

"Oh, stop it," she said. "Tell me I haven't tied myself to a human romantic. I get enough of that shit from those two." She mock-glared at the pair still embracing on the lawn. Temple grinned even wider, a laugh bubbling up from his chest.

⸺◆⸺

That evening, after everyone had been installed in the old farmhouse and treated to a memorable meal courtesy of Vella and Karden, their elderly hosts, Temple sat outside on the wraparound porch, watching darkness steal across the fields. Ryder had gone to take a look at Vella's knee, which had been giving her trouble for the last few months. The others had either retired or were chatting with Karden about the latest news from the northern continent.

After several minutes of having the porch to himself, Temple heard a door open and the scuff of a footfall. He turned to find Ash standing a few steps away, looking out into the deepening dusk.

"It's quiet out here," Temple said.

"Disconcertingly so, yes," Ash replied. He was silent for a moment before continuing, "I can only stay for a couple of days. My situation back in the Capital is… complicated. But I wanted to come here with the rest of you for a specific purpose. I'm about to overstep my bounds rather significantly, and in a way that might well backfire on me in spectacular fashion. I thought you should know ahead of time, but I don't want to say more. This way, if I've made the wrong decision, you at least will have plausible deniability."

Temple stared at him. "Er… okay. Cryptic, much?" he asked.

Ash didn't smile. "Rather frequently, I'm afraid."

"Whatever. Just be aware that if you do anything to hurt either Ryder or Skye, you'll be needing that laser pistol you keep under your pillow."

"Noted."

Temple frowned, watching Ash retreat back into the house, and wondering what in the hell he was up to.

TWENTY

Ryder spent the first day on Karden and Vella's farm trying to decide if she liked the rural surroundings or not. There was no denying it was beautiful here, but by the afternoon following their arrival, she'd decided it was, in fact, driving her a bit mad.

Once she'd unpacked their meager belongings and helped Hunter and Pax camouflage the fighters, the only thing Ryder had to occupy her time was a quick consultation with Vella about her recent knee pain, for which she'd suggested a regimen of stretching and strengthening exercises.

She'd spent the night wrapped once more in Temple's arms, after a couple of extremely enjoyable hours spent exploring the various ways a male human and a female Vithii might fit together. After so long on her own, it was seriously tempting to simply lock Temple in the bedroom and drown her sorrows using his body... but it would be blatantly obvious what they were doing in the old, thin-walled house, and it seemed a bit disrespectful to their hosts.

Karden had given her a surprised look that morphed into curiosity when Temple had first requested a room with a single bed. He still seemed a bit taken aback whenever he saw them together, but to his credit, he hadn't said a word to her. Evidently, the debt he and his mate owed Kade extended as far as being polite to a *grei'kaapt* female who was fucking a human man under his roof.

Unfortunately, the less Ryder had to occupy her mind, the more she started to think… and to remember. Remembering the past was not something she was in a hurry to do these days. While it was hardly fair to blame Temple, the reality was that her late-night confession to him and Ash, combined with the siege he'd levied against her defensive walls, meant that her emotions were dangerously close to the surface right now.

Add to that the shameful secret she was still hiding from the others, and… *well*. She was a damned mess, to put it mildly. Things had been considerably simpler when she could just hide inside her shell, throwing barbs at the world whenever it dared to get too close.

Since she'd decided that holding Temple hostage in the little attic bedroom they'd been given wasn't a viable option, she was curled up with him on the battered sofa in the living room instead. She'd dozed a bit, which was good. Dozing precluded thinking. Maybe she would ask their hosts if they had a wine cellar. Alcohol also precluded thinking—at least, it did if you drank enough of it.

It was very quiet inside the house. She wondered if the others had gone out somewhere while she was napping. She rested against Temple's side, enjoying the feeling of his fingers trailing idly up and down her arm, the motion rhythmic and relaxing. She was just contemplating closing her eyes again when Pax entered. He was dressed somberly, and she briefly considered asking where the funeral was before deciding that the quip would be wasted on him.

Ah, gallows humor. The one saving grace of the medical profession.

"Come with me, please," Pax said without preamble. "Both of you."

Ryder frowned, and felt Temple go still beside her, his fingers stopping their slow movement over her skin.

"Why?" she asked, already rising. "What's going on?"

Pax headed for the front door and she followed, Temple only a step behind her.

"I will explain when we get where we're going," the cyborg said over his shoulder. "It is approximately half a kilometer from here."

Ryder threw a glance at Temple, who shrugged, looking as confused as she was. Pax led them down a dirt track leading through a field of waving grain.

"Is someone hurt?" she pressed. "Should I have brought a medical kit?"

"I'm led to believe it's an old injury," Pax said—his voice, as ever, giving away nothing. "A medical kit is not necessary."

He turned onto a side trail that disappeared into a wooded area. Their surroundings were beautiful. It was another perfect late summer day, and the faint breeze ruffled the branches of the conifers, making them rustle. The sound of trickling water reached her ears—a rarity on the dry northern continent, but common in the agricultural lands of the south. The woods opened onto a glade of uncultivated native grasses, dominated by a massive *chik'taap* tree growing from the bank of a babbling stream.

The others were waiting under its branches, dressed as soberly as Pax in dark, unornamented colors. Ryder stumbled to a halt, feeling her heart rate and breathing quicken only an instant before she noticed the collection of stone markers dotting the ground beneath the canopy of the old tree. Temple's hands closed around her upper arms, steadying her.

"Come, Ryder," Pax said, implacable. "Your family is waiting for you."

She didn't want to go any closer. She didn't want to see whatever was waiting for her under that tree. But her feet stumbled forward anyway, step by slow step. The others were silent. Somber.

One of the stones was newer than the rest. It was un-weathered; its carved corners smooth and sharp. Her feet carried her closer to it, until she could read the inscription.

Eldrin Erisuel
Beloved Son
11/28/12—13/17/14

Ryder's knees gave out, and she crumpled to the ground, Temple supporting her on the way down. A horrible, terrifying, out-of-control feeling started to rise beneath her ribcage, squeezing out the air until there was no room for anything except a mother's grief, denied for eight long, lonely years.

"Did you know about this?" she asked Temple, the words barely more than shapes in the air as the boulder lodged inside her chest pressed down on her lungs.

"No," he said. "No, Red. I didn't."

Ash knelt in front of her, gathering her numb hands between his slender, long-fingered ones. "He didn't, Ryder. I didn't tell him."

She stared at the human who had been their ally for so long. "You told the rest of them," she croaked. "You told them about—"

"I told them about your son, who died tragically of an incurable disease… and who you loved as only a mother can, but never mourned," Ash said firmly.

"Oh, *Red*," Temple murmured, and Ash let her hands slide free as he drew her close, pressing her against him.

A soft noise rose from Ryder's throat, growing louder and stronger until she was wailing her grief into Temple's chest—the grief she hadn't dared unleash for fear that it would never, ever be exhausted. Temple rocked her in his arms, pressing his lips against her hair, curling his body around her protectively as she shrieked and howled out her heartbreak.

Behind her, the keening cry of other Vithii voices joined with hers to mourn the passing of a loved one. Ryder screamed and screamed until her voice finally failed her. The others never stopped in their mourning cries… never left her voice to grieve alone.

When she could go on no longer, she slumped, shuddering in Temple's arms. Around her, the other voices went quiet as well, the echoes fading until only the breeze and the babbling brook remained. Still, Temple held her, rocking her against him with tiny movements, whispering words of sorrow and comfort against her ear. She realized Ash hadn't moved from his place kneeling next to them when a second pair of human arms closed around her from behind, pressing her between his body and Temple's.

"You're allowed to grieve," he whispered. "You're allowed to hurt, Ryder."

He drew away after a long moment, and Temple urged her to rise on unsteady feet. She turned to see the others lined up, waiting patiently for her to regain enough control to acknowledge them. Hunter came forward, and Temple kept a grounding hand on her back as the leader of the Shadow Wing eased her into a close embrace.

Hunter's deep voice rumbled against her cheek where she rested against his chest, not a hint of distaste or aversion audible as he wrapped powerful arms around her and held her to him. "Your brothers and sister mourn with you, Ryder. We have always been here for you, waiting for the day when you were ready to reach out to us."

Skye was next, standing on tiptoe and pulling Ryder down enough to whisper in her ear, "I'm so sorry, Ryder. I bet he was an amazing kid, with a mother like you. I wish I could have met him."

Then came Draven, practically engulfing her in a tight hug. "Never thought I'd get a chance to do this without risking several important body parts," he told her. "But I'm sorry it took something like this to make it happen."

Kade stepped into her personal space like a shadow, his arm around her light and undemanding. "Failing to take advantage of available resources is bad strategy," he said in a low voice. "Don't make that mistake again, Ryder."

Finally, only Pax stood before her. "You don't have to—" she began, only for his steel-corded arms to close around her, holding her as though she were made of glass.

"No," he said. "I don't have to. I choose to. I cannot grieve with you, Ryder… but I can stand at your side while *you* grieve. You should honor your pain, my sister. To hide and deny it is an insult, though I'm certain you did not intend it as such. Your son deserves to be mourned by his family."

Pax held her for a long moment before letting her go. When he finally did, she moved slowly back to the fresh memorial stone and knelt in front of it, tracing the inscription with a fingertip.

"I tried to save him," she said, softly, but still audible to everyone gathered around her. "I was a doctor, and I tried to save him, but in the end I only added to his suffering. How does a mother go on after that? How do I let it go?"

Temple knelt with her again, his arm wrapping around her shoulders. She leaned into him, still letting her gaze play over the carved name, and its companion words. *Beloved son.*

"You don't let it go, Ryder. You hold it close, and remember, and do good things in his name for the rest of your life to honor his loss. And whenever it becomes too much, you lean on the people who love you, until you're strong enough to stand again. Your family is here for you. I… am here for you. You're not in this alone. To be honest, I don't think you ever were."

The idea circled restlessly, refusing to settle. To be *grei'kaapt* was to always be alone. Yet here she knelt, in the arms of a man who had claimed her and promised never to let her go—society be damned. Her skin still tingled with warmth from the comforting embrace of five brothers and a sister who cared nothing about her supposed untouchability in the face of her grief.

She was *grei'kaapt*… but she was not alone.

"Thank you," she breathed. "I don't know how to…" She paused, swallowing hard. "I… don't know what to say."

Temple squeezed her tight against him. "Yes you do, Red. You just said it."

The eight of them stayed there until the sun began to slip past the horizon, standing under the chik'taap tree with the gravestones as the sunset painted everything around them purple and gold.

Silent. Safe. *Together.*

EPILOGUE

Pax sat in a comfortable chair on the porch of the remote farmhouse, his enhanced senses cast outward into the night. He had no expectation that anyone or anything would intrude on his comrades' refuge, nor did he have any expectation that it wouldn't. It cost him little to tie his internal systems into the sensors of Hunter and Kade's two-seat fighters, both hidden in the field next to the house. So that's what he did.

Kade sat next to him, holding a glass tumbler containing some sort of alcoholic beverage. Pax had not taken note of the label on the dusty bottle, but whatever it was, it contained approximately thirty-eight percent ethanol by volume, and had roughly the same bouquet as industrial solvent. As was generally the case, Kade was not actually *drinking* the spirits—merely cradling the glass in his hands.

Pax had once attempted to design an algorithm to predict whether Kade would ignore the danger to his remaining brain cells by consuming alcohol in any given situation. As a neurotonin addict, ethanol consumption was potentially far more destructive to him than it was to a healthy Vithii male of his age and weight. Sometimes, however, that knowledge did not seem to be enough to stay his hand.

When the situation was not immediately threatening, Kade merely held his alcoholic beverage and stared at it from time to time. When he had access to spirits and there was imminent danger to life and limb, he took three careful swallows and put the rest aside.

On one of the two occasions during which Kade had believed Hunter to be dead, he'd gotten blind drunk and staggered into the common room where Pax and the others had been gathered, rambling on about a convoluted and unlikely scenario involving Hunter's means of escape from certain death. A convoluted and unlikely scenario, Pax hastened to add, which had turned out to be absolutely true. Without Kade's drunken epiphany, the rest of them never would have been able to find and retrieve Hunter from his hiding place inside a decompressing storage container in time to keep him from suffocating.

On the other occasion Kade had believed Hunter to be dead, he'd thrown the only bottle of booze on the station against the wall, shattering it. That time, Ash had been the one to realize Hunter had survived.

In the end, Pax had given up his self-indulgent little mental exercise, deciding that there were simply too many variables to make an algorithm practical.

"We need to find some way to leverage Ryder's new contact—that Vitharan ambassador from the prison," Kade said, breaking the silence.

"Agreed," Pax replied.

"I wish I understood what her angle was, though," Kade continued.

Pax remained silent, having no immediate insights into the matter.

"I mean, a Vitharan observer inside the Ilarian criminal justice system after that debacle with the bioweapon… that makes sense," said Kade. "But a half-Maelfian Vitharan observer with undisclosed telepathic abilities? To me, that says *espionage*."

Pax shrugged, neither agreeing nor disagreeing as Kade continued to think aloud.

"Add that to the contact Ash is trying to arrange, and we start to see some real clout that could be turned against the Premiere. That has to become our primary focus. We won't win this battle with prison riots and guerilla strikes. It will have to be a political victory. We need offworld alliances."

"There is an unacceptably high risk that Ash will be killed before he is successful in his mission," Pax observed.

"Ash has more lives than a human cat," Kade muttered.

Pax glanced at him, frowning. "Ash has the same number of lives as any other human or Vithii. One."

"It's a metaphor, Pax," Kade said pointedly.

"It is an unnecessary example of hyperbole," Pax retorted, "and has no value to the current situation."

In the distance, he registered the heat signature of a native *fehlat*-deer emerging from the woods to feed in the grain fields.

"If he can gain the ear of the human ambassador to Vithara, though…" Kade began.

"Then it would be very helpful, yes," Pax finished. "And if he dies before that happens, it would be very *unhelpful*."

Kade sighed. "It's getting late. Certain you don't want someone to take a watch later?"

"I am certain."

The other Vithii got to his feet and pushed the tumbler into Pax's hands. "Drink this for me," he said. "It's too old and valuable to waste."

Pax knocked back the foul-tasting stuff, knowing the bots in his bloodstream would immediately break it down into simple sugars for fuel. He handed the tumbler back without comment.

"Right. I'm going to bed," Kade informed him. "Hopefully everyone inside who's inclined that way will have already fucked themselves into exhaustion and fallen asleep."

Pax didn't have the heart to mention the rhythmic thumping of a bed frame and increasingly loud moans he could detect coming from Hunter and Skye's room.

"Goodnight, Kade."

Kade waved a careless hand in lieu of an answer and disappeared inside, leaving Pax alone with the night and the distant *fehlat*-deer. He sat, thinking about Ryder and considering the complexities of Vithii emotions. He was pleased that she had finally allowed herself closure of a sort, and even more pleased that she had opened her mind to the idea of coupling with a suitable individual despite her unfortunate bonding situation.

For as long as he had known her, Ryder had been haunted by a decision made in the throes of a mother's fear for her child's life. He had theorized that her failure to save her son lay at the root of her tenacious, years-long quest to master the technology of the nanobots that maintained and bolstered Pax's systems. While he would never wish the loss of a child on anyone, least of all one of his few friends, the reality was that without Ryder's presence and know-how, both Hunter and Skye would be dead now, as would the majority of the humans living in the Capital, after the Premiere's bio-attack.

He hoped she realized that. Perhaps he would point it out to her, once she'd had a bit more time to devote to her emotional and physical recovery.

Deep in Pax's systems, a connection flicked on, making him pause in his idle ponderings. He went very still, focusing inward on the unexpected signal flashing a complicated code along the embedded cybertech winding through his synapses. A complicated—and very *familiar*—code. One that his logic functions insisted must be a malfunction, since its presence was impossible.

That code was D-8's distress beacon. A call for help from one of his fellow cyborgs.

A cyborg that should not exist.

D-8 was dead.

Pax had stood motionless in a spotless laboratory some seven years ago... and seen D-8 decommissioned and vaporized with his own eyes.

finis

The *Love and War* series continues with Book 3: *Antibody*.

To discover more books by this author, visit www.rasteffan.com

www.ingramcontent.com/pod-product-compliance
Lightning Source LLC
Chambersburg PA
CBHW031008190726
48286CB00003BA/748